물 향기 수목원

Arboretum of Water Fragrance

물 향기 수목원 *Arboretum of Water Fragrance*

2026년 01월 30일 초판 1쇄 인쇄 발행

e-mail	K01045391337@daum.net
지은이	권영주
번역	라이채
펴낸이	박종래
펴낸곳	도서출판 명성서림

등록번호	301-2014-013
주소	04625 서울시 중구 필동로 6 (2, 3층)
대표전화	02)2277-2800
팩스	02)2277-8945
이메일	msprint8944@naver.com

값 22,000원
ISBN 979-11-7439-077-6

물 향기 수목원
Arboretum of Water Fragrance
시향 권영주 한영시집
라이채 번역

시집을 만드는 마음

시인은 사물을 깊이 느낄 수 있고 공감할 수 있고 혼자만이 느낄 수 있는 것을 글로써 표현한다는 것, 희로애락을 느낄 수 있다는 것을 표현해냄으로써 스트레스도 풀고 자연과 더불어 삶의 오묘한 맛도 느낄 수 있는 것입니다. 혼자만의 고독도 즐길 줄 알고 산다는 게 얼마나 감사한지 모릅니다.

인생은 어차피 잠시 쉬어가는 나그네길이지만 인간은 글을 남기고 짐승은 가죽을 남긴다고 했습니다. 그러므로 순간순간의 감정을 글로써 수놓아 본다는 게 얼마나 감사하며 살아있다는 것 그 자체만으로도 행복한 것입니다. 남은 삶도 그 어떤 보석보다도 빛나게 갈고 닦으면서 열심히 살아갈 것입니다. 언제나 25시를 맞이하는 마음으로 순결한 여인의 진실된 삶을 살 것이라고 다짐해 봅니다.

시는 내 마음의 절절한 영혼의 노래입니다. 사랑의 숨결로 피어나는 꿈이고 샘솟는 희망이며 아픔과 고통의 아름다움이 되기까지 피가 되어 흐르고 사랑이 가득한 뿌리와 줄기의 생명수가 되기도 합니다.

이 글이 많은 사람들의 가슴에 와 닿았으면 참 좋겠습니다. 그러므로 감동을 느낄 수 있다면 더 좋고요. 다들 열심히 읽고 항상 건강과 행운이 깃들기를 기도 드립니다.

마지막 가는 을사년을 떠나보내고 병오년(2026)을 맞이할 즈음
시향 권영주 올림

The Art of Creating a Poetry Collection

A poet feels deeply, empathizes, and gives voice to what only the poet can sense. In shaping joy, sorrow, and delight into words. Poetry eases the heart and reveals the life's mystery in harmony with nature. To cherish solitude is to know the true gift of living.

Life is but a brief traveler's road, yet it is said that while animals leave behind their hides, humans leave words behind. To weave fleeting emotions into writing is a blessing, and to live at all is happiness. I will polish my days, so they shine brighter than any jewel and strive to live sincerely with a woman's heart open to the twenty-fifth hour.

Poetry is the song of my soul. It is a dream blossoming with the breath of love, the spring of hope that wells up, and the beauty born of sorrows and pains. It flows like blood within me and becomes the living-water that nourishes love's roots and stems.

May these words touch many hearts. If they could wake even a spark of feeling, that is enough. May every reader find joy and may health and fortune dwell with you always.

Bidding farewell to the Eulsa Year and

Welcoming the Byeongo Year(2026)

Sihyang Kwon Young-Joo

저자약력

시향 권영주

1. 부산 출생

2. 여중시절, 여고시절 문학소녀임

3. 부산 경성대학교 국어교육학과 졸업

4. 현재 한국 문인 교수 겸 문학지도사

5. DPPI 대한 언론인 전문 기자 협회 편집위원장

6. 여고 2학년때 한국 문인협회 시, 수필 신인문학상 수상 등단

7. 1997년 11월 문예사조 시, 수필 등단

8. 2011년 한국 현대문학 100주년 기념 문학 대상 수상

9. 2016년 평론 등단(언론문학 특별 최고대상 수상)

10. 2016년 시, 수필 평론 명인 특별 최고대상 수상

11. 2016년 한국문화예술 특별 최고대상 수상

12. 2016년 동포문학상 수상

13. 2020년 한국문인상 수상

14. 2015년 구미 문학상 수상 외

15. 2012년 한국을 빛낸 인물 특별 최고대상(한국문학, 해외문학 발전위원) 수상

16. 2022년 1948년도 노벨문학상 수상자 T.S. 엘리엇 134주년 현대시 기념문학 대상 수상

17. 2023년 한국 힐링문학 대상 수상

18. 2023년 윤동주 기념 문학 대상 수상

19. 2024년 재능시 낭송 지도자 은상 수상

20. 2025년 김소월 문학 본상 대상 수상 외 다수 수상

21. 사)국제 펜 한국본부 전통 문화 위원회 위원

22 사)한국 문인협회 전통 문학 연구 위원회 위원

23. 한국 문예춘추 지도 위원

24. 문학과 비평 이사

25. 종로문협 이사

26. 성폭력, 가정폭력 카운슬링

27. 에어로빅 강사 지도교수

28. 펜 리더십 교육과정 이수

★ 저서 ; 『심천(深泉) 청정수』『시와 언어예술의 만남 애송시 낭송 시집』『송년의 노래』
　　『사랑배』『물 향기 수목원』 외 저서 다수

Author Profile

Sihyang Kwon Young-Joo

1. Born in Busan

2. A literature-loving girl during her middle and high school years

3. Graduated from the Department of Korean Language Education, Kyungsung University, Busan.

4. Currently professor, literary mentor, and member of the Korea Writers' Association

5. Editor-in-Chief, DPPI (Korea Professional Journalists Association)

6. Debuted in literature as a high school sophomore, receiving the New Writers' Award (Poetry and Essay) from the Korean Writers' Association

7. Officially debuted in poetry and essays in *Munye Sajo*(November 1997)

8. Awarded the Korean Modern Literature Centennial Prize(2011)

9. Began literary criticism career in 2016 (Special Grand Prize in Media Literature)

10. Awarded the Special Grand Prize in Poetry, Essays, and Criticism(2016)

11. Awarded the Special Grand Prize in Korean Culture and Arts(2016)

12. Recipient of the Dongpo Literature Prize(2016)

13. Awarded the Korea Writers' Award(2020)

14. Awarded the Gumi Literary Prize(2015) and others

15. Named among the Figures Who Brightened Korea for contributions to Korean and overseas literature(2012)

16. Recipient of the T.S. Eliot 134th Anniversary Modern Poetry Award(2022)
    — T.S. Eliot, winner of the 1948 Nobel Prize in Literature

17. Awarded the Korean Healing Literature Prize(2023)

18. Awarded the Yun Dong-Ju Memorial Literary Prize(2023)

19. Awarded the Jaeneung Poetry Recitation Silver Prize(2024)

20. Recipient of the Kim Sowol Grand Literary Prize(2025), among many other honors

21. Member, Korean PEN Traditional Culture Committee

22. Member, Korean Writers' Association Traditional Literature Research Committee

23. Advisory Board Member, Korea *Munyechunchu*

24. Director, Literature and Criticism

25. Director, Jongno Writers' Association

26. Counselor in sexual violence and domestic violence prevention

27. Certified aerobics instructor and trainer

28. Completed Fun Leadership training program

★ Publications: 『Deep Spring Water』 『Poetry and Language Arts : Favorite Poems Recited』 『Song of the Year's End』 『Love Ship』 『Arboretum of Water Fragrance』 and many others.

머리글 *Perface* ... 04

저자약력 *Author Profile* ... 06

1부

물 향기 수목원
Arboretum of Water Fragrance

물 향기 수목원 *Arboretum of Water Fragrance* ... 16

당신 있음에 • 1 *Because You Are • 1* ... 20

당신 있음에 • 2 *Because You Are • 2* ... 22

고향산천 그리워 *Longing for My Hometown* ... 24

온천장 벚꽃길 *Cherry Blossom Path at Oncheonjang* ... 28

산장에 비 내리다 *Rain Falling on the Mountain Lodge* ... 30

열여덟 유관순 열사의 그날은 ... 32
　　　　- 천년의 꽃 -
The Day of Eighteen-Year-Old Martyr Yoo Gwan-sun
　　- A Thousand-Year Flower -

비 오는 날의 삶의 연가 *Ballad of Life on a Rainy Day* ... 36

뻐꾸기 *Cuckoo* ... 38

동행 *Companionship* ... 40

섬진강 *Seomjin River* ... 42

바위섬 *Rocky Island* ... 44

겨울 산 *Winter Mountain* ... 46

존재의 가치 *Value of Existence* ... 48

지구촌 풍경 *Scenery of the Global Village* ... 50

가을 달빛 바람 *Autumn Moonlight Breezes* ... 52

유월의 축제 *Festival in June* ... 54

꽃향기, 글 향기 *Scents of Flowers, Scents of Words* ... 56

2부

봄꽃 여인
Lady of Spring Blossom

봄꽃 여인 *Lady of Spring Blossom* — 60

운전 길 *While Driving* — 62

봄이 온다 *Spring Is Coming* — 64

어둠 속에서의 진보 *Progress in the Dark* — 66

봄 동산 - 해동 - *Spring Hill - Thaw -* — 68

선물 *Gift* — 72

사랑배 *Love Ship* — 74

파전 *Pajeon Korean scallion pancake* — 78

가을 햇빛 속으로 *Into the Autumn Sunlight* — 80

가을입니다 *It Is Autumn* — 82

행복 길 *Path of Happiness* — 84

들국화 *Wild Chrysanthemum* — 86

마른 기침 *Dry Cough* — 88

코스모스 *Cosmos* — 90

민들레꽃•1 *Dandelion • 1* — 92

민들레꽃•2 *Dandelion • 2* — 94

불면의 가을밤 사이로 *Through a Sleepless Autumn Night* — 96

3부

노을빛 가을 거리
Autumn Street in Twilight

할미꽃·1 *Psqueflower · 1*	102
할미꽃·2 *Pasqueflower · 2*	104
낙동강 *Nakdong River*	106
에스프레소 *Espresso*	108
해운대 바다 - 열애일기 - *Haeundae Sea - Diary of Passion -*	110
초원에 누워 *Lying on the Meadow*	112
갈대 *Reeds*	114
노을빛 가을 거리 *Autumn Street in Twilight*	116
장미·1 *Rose · 1*	118
장미·2 *Rose · 2*	120
장미·3 *Rose · 3*	122
형광등 *Fluorescent Light*	124
단풍잎 *Maple Leaf*	126
별꽃 *Starflower*	128
참나무 *Oak Tree*	130
금오산·1 - 채미정 - *Mount Geumosan · 1 - Chaemijeong -*	134
금오산·2 - 호숫가 - *Mount Geumosan · 2 - By the Lakeside -*	136
금오산·3 - 올레길 - *Mount Geumosan · 3 - Olle Trail -*	138

4부

신선놀음
A Divine Amusement

물안개•1 *Mist • 1* — 142

물안개•2 *Mist • 2* — 144

연꽃 차 *Lotus Tea* — 146

자화상 *Self-Portrait* — 148

석류•1 *Pomegranate • 1* — 150

석류•2 *Pomegranate • 2* — 152

그리움•3 *Longing • 3* — 154

가을 산 *Autumn Mountain* — 156

귀가 *Homecoming* — 158

동백이 눈뜨는 날 *When Camellias Open Their Eyes* — 162

달 *Moon* — 164

세상 기슭 *Edge of the World* — 166

네가 가던 그날은 *The Day You Left* — 168

혼자 우는 바다 *Sea Weeping Alone* — 170

신선놀음 *A Divine Amusement* — 172

시인의 꿈 *A Poet's Dream* — 174

연인 *Lovers* — 176

생명•1 *Life • 1* — 178

5부

숨어 우는 바람 소리에
The Weeping Wind In Hiding

시인의 마음 *The Poet's Heart* — 182

바람 부는 날 *A Windy Day* — 184

초승달•1 *Crescent Moon • 1* — 186

초승달•2 *Crescent Moon • 2* — 188

오월의 철쭉 *Pink Azaleas of May* — 190

그 한 사람 *That One Person* — 192

꽃과 물 *Flowers And Water* — 194

숨어 우는 바람 소리에•1 *The Weeping Wind In Hiding • 1* — 196

숨어 우는 바람 소리에•2 *The Weeping Wind In Hiding • 2* — 198

송년의 노래 *Song of the Year's End* — 200

아스팔트가의 단풍나무들 *Maple Trees on the Asphalt Road* — 202

동백꽃•1 *Camellia • 1* — 206

동백꽃•2 *Camellia • 2* — 208

동백꽃•3 *Camellia • 3* — 210

동백꽃•4 - 생강나무 - *Camellia • 4 - Spicebush -* — 212

님이시여, 때가 왔습니다 *Beloved, the Time Has Come* — 214

봄빛 건배 잔 *Toasting Glass of Spring Light* — 218

당신 앞에선 *Before You* — 220

보낼 수 없는 그대 *The One I Cannot Let Go* — 222

지난날은 별이 되었다 *Bygone Days Become Stars* — 224

속삭임 *Whisper* — 226

나의 문학관
My Poetic Vision

◆◆◆

나의 문학관 *My Poetic Vision*   230

문학과 철학 *Literature and Philosophy*   232

서평
Commentary

◆◆◆

서평 | 마침내 꽃이 되다 *At Last, Becoming a Flower*   238

역자 후기 *Translator's Note*   276

역자 약력 *Translator Profile*   280

1부

물 향기 수목원
Arboretum of Water Fragrance

물 향기 수목원

모처럼 너를 찾아간 길
고운 햇살에 바람이 곱다

햇살도 숨을 몰아쉬며
계절의 강을 건넌다
모처럼 너를 찾아간 길

수양버들 진달래 명자꽃
왼 주머니에 바람을 넣고
오른 주머니에 웃음꽃을
숨겨와

봄볕이 들면 모두 꺼내어
진달래 웃고 있는 그 곳에
산으로 엄마와 진달래 꽃향기를
마시러 간다

진달래꽃이 가득 배부르면
가슴에 달고 계시는 엄마를
연분홍 꽃잎이 육자배기를
구성지게 불러준다

엄마는 반짝이는 봄볕에 나와서
갖은 양념으로 버무려 맛있게 무쳐낸다
봄 햇살 밥과 더불어 한껏 맛이 있었다.

Arboretum of Water Fragrance

The road I take at last to visit you
The sunlight tender the wind fair

The sunlight too catching its breath
Crosses the river of the seasons
The road I take at last to visit you

Weeping willows azaleas quince blossoms
I hide
Wind in my left pocket
Flower of laughter in my right

When spring sunlight pours I draw them forth
Into the mountains where azaleas smile
With my mother I climb
To drink the fragrance of their bloom

When azaleas fill us to the brim

My mother adorned her breast with flowers

I sing Yukjabaegi in a soulful voice

Calling *Pale Pink Petals*

My mother comes out into the shining spring sunlight

Mixing all the seasonings into a dish full of flavor

It tasted so delicious with the rice of spring sunlight.

당신 있음에 • 1

아름다움과 그리움의 별들이
가득 찬 희망으로
사랑으로, 행복으로
하늘과 바다와 땅의 이름으로
가슴을 채울 수 있어
고개 들고 웃음으로 빛나는
당신 있음에
내 어찌 기뻐하지 않겠는가?

내 가슴 채울 수 있는 당신 앞에선
괴로움도 사치라 할 수 있어
홀로 이길 수 있는 연습도 하고
언제나 당신 앞에선 당당하게
삶의 의욕과 어떤 아픔도, 고난도, 비난도
감당하며 기쁨으로 만발한
함박꽃 웃음으로
찬란히 빛나리라.

Because You Are • 1

Stars of beauty and longing

Brimming with hope

With love, with happiness

In the name of sky sea and earth

My heart can be filled

With your head lifted shining in a smile

Because you are here

How could I not rejoice?

Before you who can fill my heart

Even sorrow could be called a luxury

I practice to endure alone

Yet always before you I stand unafraid

Bearing the will to live and every pain

Hardship trial or blame

Blooming fully with joy

With a radiant smile

I will shine brilliantly.

당신 있음에·2

당신이 있어 행복 꽃 피고
내가 있어 사랑 꽃 피어
일렁이는 창가에 기대어
마음속 애기하며
꽃 필 수 있어 좋다.

마냥 가슴에 품고
행복 꽃, 사랑 꽃, 사랑의 비밀
고운 꽃 들판 당신 가슴 숨결처럼
가을로 올 수 있을까?

웃을 수 있는 고운 나비꽃처럼
예쁘고 아름다운 당신 가슴
하냥 행복 흐른다.

시간(時間)의 꽃을 가슴에 품고
행복 꽃, 사랑 꽃, 당신 가슴 숨결처럼
고운 꽃 들판 가을 향기 가득
꽃향기 가슴 피우리라.

당신 있음에·2

Because You Are • 2

Because of you flowers of happiness bloom

Because of me flowers of love bloom

Leaning by the shimmering window

Blooming with cheerful talk

Whispered from my heart.

Holding close within my heart

Flowers of happiness, flowers of love, the secret of love

A gentle field of blossoms like the breath in your chest

Could it return again as autumn?

Like a graceful butterfly-flower smiling

Your heart so lovely and beautiful

Lets happiness flow without end.

With the flowers of time held to my heart

Flowers of happiness, flowers of love, like the breath in your chest

In a gentle field filled with autumn fragrance

The scent of blossoms will bloom in my heart.

고향산천 그리워

아련한 추억의 푸념은
예정 없이
하루를 꼬박 서성이다
지친 듯

종달새 울음
그 언덕에도 애꿎은
상념만 보내고 나니

커다랗게 피어난
들풀의 흔들거림이
마지막 인사치레로
넘실댄다

그리움은 핑계처럼 돌아가버리고
세월의 무게들만 라일락 잎새
스치듯 휘어돌아
묵은 피를 토해내고

흔적을 찾아
빗방울에 실어봅니다.

Longing for My Hometown

The rambling lament of the faded memories

Unplanned

Has me wandering all day

And

I let it go as if worn out

The lark's cry

Even on that hill

Only sends off pointless thoughts

The wide blooming sway of

Wild grass ripples

In a final gesture of farewell

Longing turns back like an excuse

And only the weight of years

Brushes past lilac leaves in a winding arc

Spits out the clotted blood

In search of traces

I set them afloat on raindrops.

온천장 벚꽃길

봄 햇살, 바람 따가워
벚꽃 나무 잎새들

연분홍 양산을 쓰고
핑크빛 립스틱 웃음 지으며
양 길가에 모두들 나와
나를 환호한다.

온천천 맑은 물살
작은 물고기떼들
백조 물새 되어 날며

들풀 새싹 올라와
새 생명 얻고
아름다운 세상

봄 햇살 길 열렸다.

Cherry Blossom Path at Oncheonjang

In the spring sun and wind
Cherry petals quiver

With light pink parasols and
Smiles painted in rosy lipstick
They line both sides of the road
Cheering for me.

The clear current of Oncheon Stream
Small schools of fish
The swan flies becoming a water bird

Wild grass sprouts push through
Gaining new life
In this beautiful world

The path of spring sunlight has opened.

산장에 비 내리다

푸른 세포들이
저마다의 자태로
일어선다

비에 세차게
얻어맞은
푸른 나무 잎새들

촉촉한 대지위에
청춘들이 누워있다

신비에 싸인 저 오묘한 세상을
밝히려고 등불이 걸어간다

피멍 든 가지에 푸른 잎새
새롭게 돋아나
보름달처럼 환하게 웃는다.

Rain Falling on the Mountain Lodge

Green cells

Rise

Each in their own grace

The green leaves of trees

Beaten hard

By rain

On the moistened earth

Youth lies resting

A lantern walks on

To light that wondrous world

On the branches bruised with dark stains

Fresh green leaves sprout again

And smile brightly like a full moon.

열여덟 유관순 열사의 그날은

- 천년의 꽃 -

유관순, 그녀가 가던 그날은
하늘이 슬피 울고 땅도 울고
새들도 울었다.

일천구백일십구년 삼월 봄부터 이듬해 구월까지
열여덟 순국선열 유관순, 그녀는
대한독립만세! 피맺힌 절규! 절규!

온통 울음바다, 그치지 않고
마디마디 울어서 퉁퉁 부어 있었다.
못다 핀 꽃 유관순 열사, 대한독립만세!
부르짖다 간 청춘의 넋이여!

그녀가 가던 그날의 눈물이 너무 젖어
압록강 한강 낙동강 빨갛게 타올라
철철 넘쳐흘러 마침내 광복절의 해방!

민족의 가슴에는 사랑으로 희망으로
천년의 꽃이 되어 하늘 동산에
길이길이 피어났다.

The Day of Eighteen-Year-Old Martyr Yoo Gwan-sun

− A Thousand−Year Flower −

Yoo Gwan-sun,

On the day she bid her last farewell

The sky wept the earth wept and

Even the birds wept.

From the spring of March 1919

To the September of the following year

Eighteen-year-old martyr Yoo Gwan-sun,

Her cry her blood-sealed cry

Long live Korean independence!

A cry soaked in blood a cry!

A flood of sorrow, never ceasing

Every joint swelling with each sob.

Her body bruised and swollen

Yoo Gwan-sun, the flower that could not fully bloom!

O soul of youth gone shouting Long live Korean independence!

The tears of the day she left this tear soaked land

Turning the Amnok River the Han River and

The Nakdong River burning red

Overflowing until at last came the Liberation Day of freedom!

In the heart of the nation as love and as hope

She became a flower of the Thousand Years

Forever blooming

In the heavenly garden.

비 오는 날의 삶의 연가

비 오는 날
속살 여미며 새벽을 흔들어
깨우는 그리움으로
젖어든 가슴팍 한가운데

삶의 연주는
소나기 퍼붓는 선율 따라
핏빛 소망으로 둥지를 튼다

지고한 목숨의 연원으로 자리매김한
님의 황홀한 언저리

여명의 종소리는
풋풋한 사랑의 체온으로
닻을 내리며

저 건강한 부활의 아침을 맞는다.

Ballad of Life on a Rainy Day

On a rainy day

Longing gathers my tender flesh and

Shakes the dawn and awake

In the soaked center of my heart

The music of life

Nests in the crimson wish

Following the melody of pouring rain

In the halo of the beloved

Who has taken root

As the origin of this noble life

The bell of daybreak

Drops anchor

In the warmth of fresh love

And greets that vigorous morning of resurrection.

뻐꾸기

애처롭게 우짖는다
뻐꾹 뻐꾹 다급해진 목소리

한번 품어 보지도 못하고
남의 보금자리에 맡기고

내 새끼 잘 있나
마음 졸이며 먼발치서
애타는 어미 마음

너는 뻐꾸기 새끼란다
뻐꾹 뻐꾹 엄마를
잊지 말아다오.

Cuckoo

Cries in sorrow

Cuckoo Cuckoo — her voice grows urgent

Without ever having held even once

Entrusting her eggs to another's nest

Are my chicks safe

The mother's heart frets

Watching anxiously from afar

You are Cuckoo chicks

Cuckoo Cuckoo

Please Do Not Forget Your Mother.

동행

서로 다른 옷을 입은 채
숨 가쁘게 가던 길

되돌아보면
아쉬움만 쌓인 아득한 길

함께한 세월이
맑은 옹달샘처럼
치솟기만 한다면!

미움 한 모금 지우고
두려움 한 모금 버리고

언제부턴가 너는 나의 날개
나는 너의 날개가 될 것이리라.

Companionship

Wearing different clothes

On this road we walked breathlessly

Looking back

It stretches far filled only with longings

If the years we shared

Would rise up

Like a fresh spring!

Erasing a sip of hatred

Casting away a sip of fear

Someday you will be my wings and

I shall be yours.

섬진강

걸어서 하늘까지 가다가 지치면
별들이 내려와 멱을 감고
맑고 투명한 이야기가 밤을 지새는

노고단 스쳐우는 바람
고독한 나그네의 생사를 넘나드는
방랑의 세월

수천, 수만리 부딪혀도
깨어지지 않고
정다운 가슴 가득 품어
산모롱이길 돌아서서

삶의 고뇌와 걱정의 분리수거를
한 겹 벗어버리고
섬진강 물줄기 굽이굽이
돌아눕는다.

Seomjin River

Walking all the way to the sky until weary
The stars come down to bathe and
Pure and guileless stories
Keep the night awake

The winds brushing past Nogodan
Crosses between life and death
For the lonely wanderer's years of roaming

Though clashing along a road of countless miles
It never breaks
But holds a heart full of affection
Turning around the mountain bends

Shedding one layer
In the sorting of life's anguish and worries
The Seomjin River's current
Turns and lies down through winding ways.

바위섬

모래바람 일으키며
둘레둘레 동백섬 돌아
피는 산 꽃

꽃바람 치솟는
태양 시심(詩心) 안고
꽃향기 불러보는
시인이 되어

하늘 우러러
파도가 부딪혀도
얼싸안고 달래는
봄 갈매기 바위섬으로
서리라.

Rocky Island

Stirring up sandy winds

Circling and circling Camellia Island

The mountain flowers bloom

With the rising flowery wind

Embracing the sun's poetic heart

I become the poet

Calling forth the fragrances of flowers

Looking up to the sky

Even as waves crash against me

I will withstand

As the rocky island for the spring gulls

That holds and soothes them in its arms.

겨울 산

바람들이 마디마디 풀어 헤쳐
오늘을 토해내고야 말았다!

돌아온 마음같이
떠나간 너의 마음이여
빛으로 사는 물결

내 가슴에도 성탑을 쌓고
오늘을 보내는
쉰 목소리가 되었다.

있으면 있는 대로
산은 말이 없고
봄, 여름, 가을도 잊고
홀로 불씨 지펴
살아가고 있다.

Winter Mountain

Winds at every branch joint unraveled
At last spat out today!

Like a heart that had returned
O heart that departed from me
Waves that live in light

I too have built a tower in my chest
And now I send off the day
With a voice gone hoarse.

If it is there it is as it is
The mountain remains silent
Forgetting spring, summer, and autumn
Alone kindling embers and
Going on with life.

존재의 가치

진솔한 얘기

여유로운 삶

아름다운 생명체

꽃향기 날릴 때

존재의 가치

행운의 생명은

소중한 사랑으로 도전한다.

Value of Existence

Sincere words

A leisurely life

A beautiful living being

When the fragrances of flowers drift

One realizes the value of the existence

A life blessed with fortune

Takes on challenges with precious love.

지구촌 풍경

하늘바다, 푸른 바다
여기저기 하얀 뭉게 꽃구름
속삭임 넘나드는
세상사 풍경!

하늘꽃 머금은 저곳엔
잠깐 머뭇거림도 없이

해 질 녘 꽃구름 사이
황금빛 들풀의 향연 속
양떼들도 내 마음 울리네

내일은 자연과 더불어
바다에 비단결 꽃무늬
마음속에 수놓아 보련다.

Scenery of the Global Village

Sky the sea, and the blue ocean

Here and there white fluffy flower-clouds

Whispers passing back and forth

Scenes from the world!

Where the sky holds its flowers

Without the slightest hesitation

At sunset among the flower-clouds

In the golden feast of wild grasses

Even the flocks of sheep stir my heart

Tomorrow together with nature

I will embroider in my heart

Silken floral patterns upon the sea.

가을 달빛 바람

달빛 바람 속에
흐르는 베토벤의 운명처럼
내 운명 폭포의 물줄기 생명수 물결
여태껏 통증을 끌어안던 삶
내려놓고 나만의 길 나만의 속삭임
엇박자의 삶

귀뚜라미 연주하던 그곳에서
싱싱한 가을 하늘 바람
벗 삼아 놀고 싶어

하루하루 그대들에게
내 마음 전하면서
새벽 기도하고 삶의 무게 안고
파닥이는 아가미 입술
부끄러운 변명 꽃 잘라내고
여명의 문 활짝 열고 들어서리라.

Autumn Moonlight Breezes

In the moonlit breezes

Like Beethoven's Fate flowing through the air

The life-giving streams from my waterfall of fate

A life that had embraced pain until now

I set it down take my own path my own whispers

A life out of rhythm

In the place where crickets once played their music

I wish to spend the day with the fresh autumn sky

And the wind as my companion

Day by day

Delivering my heart to you

Praying at dawn bearing the weight of life

With lips like fluttering gills

I will cut away the flowers of shameful excuses

And step brightly into the morning.

유월의 축제

초여름 더위가 성큼 다가올
유월의 한마당

축제는 봄에서부터
이어져왔다

늦은 겨울 칼바람 가장자리에서
봄은 그렇게 서서히 아름다움으로
성숙되어가고

이제는 붉고 푸른
초여름의 축제가 열린다

행복은 유월의 태양의 때때옷 입고
모든 사람의 발걸음을
가볍게 재촉한다.

Festival in June

With the early summer's heat
Stepping swiftly into June's grand stage

The festival has continued
Since spring

From the edge of winter's late bitter winds
Spring has slowly matured
Into beauty

And now the Red and Green
The Festival of Early Summer opens

Happiness, dressed in the rainbow-hued robe,
June's sun
Lightly hastens the steps of everyone.

꽃향기, 글 향기

적막한 하늘 아래
풀벌레들 노래 부른다.

한줄기 햇살이 휘감아 돌더니
달도 별도 나그네도
바람까지 모여 앉아
도란도란 얘기한다.

지금은 꽃향기, 글 향기에
잠시 쉬지 않고
가는구나!

고달프면 좀 쉬렴!
꽃향기, 글 향기에 취해
구름밭에 안기어
한가로이 논다.

Scents of Flowers, Scents of Words

Beneath the quiet sky

Insects sing their songs in the grass.

A single ray of sunlight swirls around

Then the moon the stars the wanderer

Even the breezes gather close and

Chat in quiet tones.

In the scents of flowers, the scents of words

I have passed without pausing

Even for a moment!

If weary then take a rest awhile!

Drunk on the scents of flowers, the scents of words

I float away into a field of clouds and

Idle away hours.

2부

봄꽃 여인
Lady of Spring Blossom

봄꽃 여인

겨울바람이 가면서

봄을 데려왔다

어느새 길을 나선 꽃잎은

봄바람 따라 살포시 춤을 추고

여인을 설레게 한다

마침내 여인은 꽃이 되었다.

Lady of Spring Blossom

As the winter wind departed

It brought along the spring

Before long, petals set out on their way

Gently dancing with the spring breeze

Stirring a lady's heart

At last, the lady became a flower.

운전 길

앗 차 실수
접촉사고 인생길

뿌리째 뽑힐 뻔 했어

하지만 이 생명
아직 빛나고 있어

성령님 당신께서
지켜 주셨습니다

감사하옵니다
예수님 이름으로!

– 아 멘 –

While Driving

O No — a sudden mishap

A fender-bender on the life's road

I almost was uprooted completely

Yet this life

Still shines with lights

Holy Spirit it was You

Who protected me

I give Thanks

In the name of Jesus!

- Amen -

봄이 온다

숨죽인 시간
긴 겨울 엄동설한에
쩌엉 쩡 파열음

숨죽인 시간에도
꽃봉오리 터질 듯 말 듯

산 너머 따라온 햇살에
아지랑이 너울너울
춤춘다

추위에
화들짝 개구리 놀란 가슴
쓸어내린다

살며시 봄은 오려나보다.

Spring Is Coming

In the hushed time

Through the bitter cold of deep winter

A sharp, cracking sounds bursting out

Even in this hushed time

Flower buds seem ready to burst

In the sunlight trailing over the mountains

Heat haze sways and

Dances in gentle waves

In the cold

A startled frog calms

Its pounding heart

And yet quietly spring seems come.

어둠 속에서의 진보

갑작스런 어둠이 드리워질 때
욕망의 그림자
현실이 미약해
환상의 나래, 집을 짓는다.

변화의 시간이 필요해
고난을 이기는 힘
우리 서로 배려하고

함박꽃 웃음의 오늘로
자아와 지위
성공으로 끌어올리자.

Progress in the Dark

When sudden darkness falls

The shadow of desires

Builds a house of fantasy

Out of the frailty of the reality.

A time of change is needed

The strength to overcome hardships and

Care for one another

In today's bright smile

Let us lift ourselves toward success

Our identities, our positions.

봄 동산 – 해동 –

겨우내 움츠렸던
마른 나무 가지들

따뜻한 봄바람이
기지개를 켜자

팔다리에 온통
반짝반짝 햇살 조각

가슴 탱탱하게 부풀어
젖몸살 심하게 앓고 있다

아직은 그 곳에 머물러
젖은 눈으로 몸을 풀더니
앓고 있는 젖몸살 쉽게 낫지가 않는다

영양실조로 핏기 없는 아기 풀은
실눈을 뜨고

어설프게 젖꼭지를 입에 문 채
눈 맞춤한다

어여쁜 새색시 참젖은
졸졸졸 인심도 좋아

바위 사이 진달래 철쭉도
달디단 동냥젖 맘껏 먹이니

눈웃음 지으며 아지랑이
풀잎 위에 하늘거린다.

Spring Hill – Thaw –

All winter long the dry tree branches

Stayed curled in upon themselves

When the warm spring breezes

Stretch and yawn

Sunlit flecks sparkle

All over their limbs

Their chests swell tight with life

Aching with the full-breasted ache of spring

Still lingering there

They loosen their bodies with tear-damped eyes

Yet the aches do not heal so easily

The baby grass pale from malnutrition

Opens its narrow eyes

Clumsily taking the nipple in its mouth

Meets the gaze

The lovely new bride full with fresh breast milk

Generously lets it flow

Even the Flame-pink Azalea flowers in

Between the rocks drink their fill

Of the sweet shared milk

Smiling with their eyes the heat haze

Shimmers above the blades of grass.

선물

거리마다 오묘하게 우러나는
젊은 날의 달콤새콤한 추억들

하지만 세월의 강(江) 건너
지금은 눈물로 얼룩진
침묵만 있고

첫사랑의 노래보다도 감미로운
세상 보는 눈을 주었고
그러나 또한
내 영혼의 눈을 주었습니다.

Gift

On every street, subtly imbued

Linger the bittersweet memories of my younger days

But beyond the river of the passing years

Now there is only silence

Stained with tears

It gave me eyes to see the world

Sweeter than the song of the first love

But also

It gave me the eyes of my soul.

사랑배

내 귀는 소라 귀
뱃고동 소리 들려온다.

뚜우……
내게로 다가오는 항구 배 안 가득

하늘에서 주신 그대 가슴 맑은 산소
비단 물결처럼 일렁이는데

사랑배! 행복, 소망, 기쁨 가득 담고서
밀물처럼 밀려오는데
파도, 바람 잠잠하다.

내 가슴 가득
온몸으로 피어나는 향기 꽃
그윽하다.

그대 그리움에 취해 지금 잠잠히
오롯이 비단물결 일렁이는 썰물처럼
가버리는데 난 어찌 하오리!

사랑배 타고 사랑 싣고
그대 가슴 꽃길 열릴 때까지
기다릴게요.

Love Ship

My ears are conch shells

Hearing the ship's horn.

Toot……

A harbor ship, full and coming toward me

The clear oxygen of your heart given from heaven

Ripples like silk waves

Love ship! Filled with happiness, hope and joy

Comes rushing in like the rising tide

While waves and wind lie still.

My heart brims with

A fragrance blooming through my whole body

Deep and rich.

Drunk on longing for you now quietly

Like the ebbing tides like silk waves ripple

But you go away and O how can I go on!

I will ride the love ship carrying love, and

I will wait until the flower path in your heart opens.

파전

결혼식 때 '검은머리 파뿌리 되도록
사랑하겠는가?'

반쯤 풀죽은 파 위에 얹혀진
오징어 조금, 청고추, 홍고추 조금 조금
익은 부위마다 덕지덕지 양념 부위들

비오는 날 새 힘, 새 행운을 빌며
건배! 축하해 행복해라.

Pajeon Korean scallion pancake

At the wedding 'Will you love each other
Until black hair turns to scallion white?'

On the half-wilted scallions are laid
A bit of squid, green chili, red chili
Seasoned bits clinging thick
To every cooked part

On a rainy day wishing for new strength, new fortune
Cheers! Congratulations Be happy.

가을 햇빛 속으로

깊은 곳으로 보냈다고
생각하겠지만
내가 사는 하늘은 하늘이 아닌
복사 빛도 아닌 지칠 수 없는 곳에 잠겼어.

내 뒤엔 접혀진 길목의 주름들
멀리 있어 좋은 가을날의 햇빛이니
지금은 보이는 대로 보지 말고
들리는 대로 듣지 마라.

혼자만이 맞이하는 나의 계절
누가 와서 벗이 되어 줄래?
깊은 질문의 답
소리 없는 소리와 싸우는 비명!

Into the Autumn Sunlight

You may think I was sent to some deep place

But the sky I live in is not the sky

Not even with reflected light

It is immersed in a place that cannot tire.

Behind me are the folded wrinkles of crossroads

It is the sunlight of the far-off autumn days so

Do not look only as it appears now

Do not listen only as it sounds.

My season welcomed in solitude

Who will come and be my friend?

The answer to a deep question

A scream wrestling with silence!

가을입니다

이태리의 사원을 맴돌다 온
착한 바람은
열 오른 대지의 이마를 식혀주며
이 가을을 당신께 선물합니다.

이제
온 천하가 울긋불긋 꽃 자락
가득 피우고 익을 대로 익어
톡톡 터지는 밤송이 비명!

인류 최초의 음악도
착한 바람 같은 비명이기에
솔직한 이 가을을
당신께 선물합니다.

It Is Autumn

The gentle breeze

That circled the temples of Italy

Cools the fevered brow of the earth

And offers this autumn to you as a gift.

Now

The whole world in crimson blossoms

Ripens to the fullest

Like chestnuts burr bursting with crackling cries!

For even the

Humanity's first music

Was a cry like the gentle wind

And so I offer this honest autumn

To you as a gift.

행복 길

철부지 어린 시절
부모의 보호막은
너무 강했다

여태껏 말없이 앞만 보고
달려왔다
이제야 힐끔 곁눈질도
하고 뒤돌아보니
덧없기만 할 뿐

가만히 보니
극복할 나만의 웃음꽃
행복은
성령안의 믿음 길 뿐이다.

- 아 멘 -

Path of Happiness

In my naive childhood

My parents' shield

Was far too strong

All this time I have run on in silence

Eyes fixed ahead

Only now do I steal a sideways glances

Looking back

Finding it all so fleeting

Taking a close look I see

The smile-blossoms, I only should nurture and overcome

Happiness

Is found only on the path of faith

In the Holy Spirit.

- Amen -

들국화

아스라한
추억 속의 그대

가을 산기슭
호젓한 호숫가
가로수 아래

차마 꺾을 수도 없는
가녀린 모습

첫사랑의 예쁜
들국화 얘기들.

Wild Chrysanthemum

You in my

Faint and distant memories

On autumn's hillside

By a solitary lakeshore

Beneath the roadside trees

Too fragile a figure

For me to ever break

Stories of my first love

Lovely wild chrysanthemum.

마른 기침

별을 쏘는 화살에
마른 기침이 돋는다

천식을 앓는 대지는
길길이 일어선다

욕심과 후회는
맨살로 울고 웃고

햇살 그리워지는 삼월의 아픔
촘촘히 파고드는데
투명한 생활 눈을 뜬다.

Dry Cough

At arrows shooting stars
A dry cough rises

The earth, wheezing with asthma
Leaps up in protest

Greed and regrets
Laughing and weeping with bare skin

The pain of March yearning for the sunlight
Pierces densely through and
A transparent life opens its eyes.

코스모스

밀물처럼 밀려오는
시간의 파도를 타고
달은 나에게로 왔다

가로등 불빛 아래
가녀린 몸짓으로

허기진 코스모스 가슴
허리마다 무심한
그리움에 젖어

뼛속까지 파고드는
고독에 몸부림친다.

Cosmos

Riding the waves of time

Surging like the rising tide

The moon came to me

Under the streetlamp's glow

With a fragile gesture

The hungry heart of the cosmos

Soaked in careless longing

Along every slender stem

Wrestles in anguish with solitude

That pierces to the bone.

민들레꽃 • 1

보도블록 위 틈새에 핀
질긴 생명 꽃
샛노랗게 피어났다.

세상살이 뭐가 좋아
틈새에서 고통을 끌어안고
피어났을까?

숨은 제대로 쉬었을까?
고개를 틀며 비집고 일어난
너의 얼굴
싱그럽게 피어났다.

휘파람으로 윙크하며
함박꽃 웃음 날린다!

Dandelion • 1

In the cracks of the sidewalk
A stubborn flower of life
Bloomed bright yellow.

What joy in this world
Made you embrace the pain and
Blossom here?

Did you ever breathe with ease?
Turning your head, pushing through
Your face emerged
Fresh in bloom.

With a whistle and a wink
You scatter smiles like blossoms!

민들레꽃 • 2

봄볕에 잠이 깨어
설렘에 눈이 부셔

제 몸 일으켜 잎을 펴고
줄기로 밀어 올린 별!

어두운 세월 견디며
땅위로 솟은 깔깔 웃는
노오란 꽃무리

대지 위에 솟아오른
노오란 별꽃들

희망으로 피어났다.

Dandelion • 2

Awakened by the spring sunlight
Dazzled with excitement

Lifting itself, opens its leaves and
Pushes up a star on its stem!

Enduring dark years
Bursting forth with laughter
A cluster of yellow flowers

Yellow Star-flowers rising
Above the earth

They have bloomed into hope.

불면의 가을밤 사이로

'고요가 세상(世上)을 넘칠 때!'

불면(不眠)을 일으켜 세우는
금빛 언어들의 수런거림에
등줄기를 타고 흘러내리는 식은 땀

진한 커피 한 잔에
머리를 식혀
입안 가득
가을을 몰고 온다.

하늘에서 하늘로
거리에서 거리로
온몸 흔들며 쏟아져 내리는
고독의 한 줄기 몸 안 가득 받아
뾰족뾰족 솟아나는 가을 새싹들처럼

그리운 꿈 향해
설렘 속 사랑으로
눈 비비며 깨어나는 햇살 한 아름
파다닥 열린 가슴으로
노랠 부른다.

Through a Sleepless Autumn Night

'When stillness overflows the world!'

The rustling of golden words
That rouse sleeplessness
Send cold sweat trickling down my spine

A strong cup of coffee
Cools my head and
Fills my mouth
With autumn's arrival.

From sky to sky
From street to street
Shaking my whole body I take in to the fullest
A stream of solitude like sharp autumn sprouts
Breaking through the earth

Toward the dreams I long for

With love in trembling excitement

A handful of sunlight rubs its eyes awake

And with a chest thrown open like wings

Sings its song.

3부

노을빛 가을 거리
Autumn Street in Twilight

할미꽃 • 1

할미꽃 호박꽃
초롱불 밝히며
일어서는 세포들

인생의 지표
아직은 힘 있다.

볼 수 있고
쓸 수 있어
얼마나 즐거운지

생의 한가운데
중심 기둥 되어
조심스레 불꽃 피운다.

Psqueflower • 1

Pasqueflower Pumpkin flower

Cells rise

Like lanterns lit

Life's compass

Still holds its strength.

To be able to see and

To be able to write

How joyful it is

In the midst of life

As a central pillar

Carefully blossoms into flames.

할미꽃 · 2

애교 섞인 미소인데
저 매혹 시샘하다 핀
눈 흘기는 할미꽃!

다소곳이 고개 숙여
영접 받아
겸손한 할미꽃
고운 자태의 봄 햇살

귀여운 수줍음에
형형색색 모르는 게 많아
상식에 어설퍼
아쉬움에 웃고 있다.

Pasqueflower • 2

With a smile tinged with charm

Blooming in envy of allure

A side-glancing Pasqueflower!

Bowing its head modestly

Welcoming with humility

The Pasqueflower

Graceful in the spring sunlight

In its shy cuteness

So much unknown in many colors

Awkward in common sense

Smiles a wistful smile.

낙동강

바람 부는 오늘도
온갖 시름안고
흐르는 낙동강

수많은 사연 속삭이듯
소곤대지만
가슴속 불덩이
타들어가

무심코 토해내어
붉게 물들이고 말았다.

Nakdong River

Today again the wind blows

Carrying every care

Flows the Nakdong River

As if whispering countless stories

Murmurs low

Yet in its heart a live ember

Burns within

Unthinkingly it exhales and

Stains the waters Red.

에스프레소

한잔의 한 모금은
눈물 젖은 한숨이다

그대의 눈물
나의 눈물
흐르는 강이 되어
세월은 흘러갔다

진정 안녕이란
말 한마디도 없이

그윽한 마지막 잎새 되어
나의 하늘로 가버렸다.

Espresso

A single sip from a single cup

Is a sigh steeped in tears

Your tears

My tears

Together became a flowing river and

Slipped away with the years

Not even a single word

Of true farewell

Became the last leaf and

Vanished into my heaven.

해운대 바다 – 열애 일기 –

가을의 옷을 벗고
님을 만나러 간다.

그 여자는
맨몸으로
맨살, 맨 허리를

감싸안는 싱싱한 달빛 바람으로
파도를 탄다.

아! 겨울바다.

Haeundae Sea − Diary of Passion −

Shedding autumn's clothes

I go to meet my beloved.

That woman

In her bare body

Her bare skin, her bare waist

By the fresh moonlit wind that wraps

Rides the waves.

Ah! The winter sea.

초원에 누워

초여름 햇살 아래
나뭇가지 싱그럽고

마음속 가로지르는
계곡 위에는
푸른 하늘에 하얀 뭉게구름꽃들
여유로움에 새들 노래하고

시간이 멈춘 것 같은 이곳
곁에 있어도
느끼지 못하던 소중한 것들

잠시 푸른 하늘의 그림 같은 집
풍경화의 동화 속 같은
열정의 꿈을 꾸었다.

Lying on the Meadow

Under the early summer sunlight

Fresh green leaves

Over the valley

Crossing my heart

White cloud-flowers in the blue sky

Birds sing in leisure

In this place where time seems to stop

The precious things

I never felt even when close by

For a moment like a house drawn in the sky

Like a fairytale within a painted landscape

I dreamed a passionate dream.

갈대

서걱대며 부비는 소리
뒤척이며 가슴 저리고

잊고 싶지 않은 기억
잊어버리는 두려움에

긴 목 휘청이며
우는 가녀린 몸짓으로
살아온 날들

기다림은 나를
흔들어놓고

투명한 바람 향기에
채워지는 보고 싶은 얼굴

저무는 들판 길 따라 흐르는
그대의 달빛 그림자!

Reeds

Rasping sound as they brush together

My heart being tossed and aches

The memories I do not wish to forget

Yet with fear of forgetting

Long neck swaying

Crying in fragile gestures

The days I have lived

Waiting shakes me

To the core

With the fragrance of transparent breezes

Fills the face I long to see

Along the fading field path flows

Your moonlit shadow!

노을빛 가을 거리

가을빛 짙은 거리엔
낮달이 나뭇가지에
걸려있고

갈색 추억 흔들리는
무지갯빛 노을
헤이즐넛 향기로
가득하다

아픔 뒹구는
빈 들녘엔
혼자라는 게
절실해지며

가도 가도 그치지 않는
푸른 생각들은
거칠게 부딪혀 오는
세상살이 숨 가빠
뼛속까지 스며드네.

Autumn Street in Twilight

Streets steeped in autumn lights
The daytime moon caught
In the branches

Brown memories swaying
Sunset glows in rainbow colors
Air filled
With hazelnut scent

In empty fields
Where sorrows roll about
The weight of being alone
So real

Endlessly pressing on
Blue thoughts will not cease
They crash against me rough and fierce
Life so breathless
It seeps into my very bones.

장미·1

기다림 없이 터질듯 숨 졸이며
무던히도 빛나는데

그대 마음 아직 요동도 않는데
진한 핏줄 터뜨리며

가시 속에 서럽도록 도도한
여인의 자태

마냥 꽃 피울 수만 있을까?

Rose • 1

Breathless as if about to burst

It shines without end in waiting

Yet your heart has not stirred

Veins break out to crimson flow

Proud yet sorrowful within thorns

The figure of a woman appears

Can it go on blooming forever?

장미·2

밖으로 화사하게 웃고
안으로 감춘 가시

너무도 달라 죽어도 타는 눈빛
애닮다 어이하리

붉은 등불 켜고 기다리다
향기에 취해

여유로운 오월의 하늘 바다에
그리움을 다 토해 낼 수 있을까?

Rose • 2

Outwardly smiles in radiant bloom

Inwardly hides its thorns

So different that with eyes burn even unto death

How aching, how helpless am I

Waiting with a red lantern lit

Drunk on its fragrance

Upon the spacious May sea in the sky

Can all this longing be poured out?

장미 • 3

장미꽃밭 속 그대의 얼굴
꽃밭에 싸여있다.

둘레둘레 웃음 자락
봄 끝자락에 휘감아
이별 노래 부르고

숨어우는 노을과 함께
초여름 가의 줄기로 앉는다.

Rose • 3

Amid the rose garden, your face

Enfolded in blossoms.

All around, trails of laughter

Entwine the edge of spring and

Sing a song of farewell

With the sunset weeping alone in hiding

It sits as a stalk on the verge of summer.

형광등

번쩍 형광등을 켜자

거울 앞에 앉아
최고로 예쁘게 화장을 한다

어둠은 거짓을 거짓되게
가르쳐 주었으나

형광 불빛은 진실대로
꾸미는 그 자체를

화려하고 예쁘게
최고의 여자로
아름답게 꾸며준다.

Fluorescent Light

Click, the fluorescent light flashes on

Sitting before the mirror
I put on makeup to be my prettiest

The darkness taught me
How falsehood makes falsehoods

The fluorescent glow shows the truth itself
Adorning is the truth of adornment

Brilliant and beautiful
Shapes me into the finest woman
And adorns me with grace.

단풍잎

선홍빛 고운 노래 목청껏 부르다
떨어진 단풍나무 잎

한목숨 왔다 가려면
부르고 또 불러
대지 위에 구르고 굴러 떠가고

마침내 뚝 그친 어느 날
하얀 겨울 눈꽃 송이
내리겠지.

Maple Leaf

Having sung its crimson song full-throated
The maple leaves fall

For a life to come and pass
It needs to sing and sing again
Rolling, tumbling, drifting across the earth

And at last on some sudden day
White blossoms of winter snow
Will fall.

127

별꽃

눈부신 별꽃이 만발한
하늘 정원에
내가 별 하나 따가려는데

하늘에서 꿈의 무지개
둥둥 하늘 높이 떠오르다가

마침내 온 세상
달과 별들의 꽃들은

새벽 텃밭에 나갔다가
길가 안개처럼 피어난 별꽃을
한 아름 안고 들어온다.

Starflower

In the garden of heaven
Dazzling Starflowers bloom in full
I reach to pluck a single star

From the heavens rises
A rainbow of dreams floating high

At last, the moon and starry blossoms
Spread through the whole world

Returning from the dawn's garden
Arms full of Starflowers blossomed
Like mist along the roadside.

참나무

언어와 음감이 예민한
참나무처럼

봄날에 눈부신
연분홍빛 인생이 출렁인다

여름엔 참나무 잎이 무성해지듯
뜨겁게 열정적으로 살고

인생의 가을엔 은은하고 맑은
황금빛 나무가 되고

마침내 겨울엔 지난날의 잎새
다 떨어지고
뿌리와 줄기만이 남은
나목이 되어

당당한 기품을 잃지 않으며
벌거벗은 참나무처럼

본연의 힘으로 굳게 지키며
살아가리라.

Oak Tree

Sensitive in language and sound
Like the oak

On spring days life glows
In dazzling light of soft pink

In summer as oak leaves grow thick
I will live ardently with passion

In autumn of life I become
A tree of golden luster gentle and clear

At last in winter all the leaves
Of the days gone by fall away
Leaving only the roots and the branches
A bare tree standing

Like the bare oak

Keeping its noble bearing

On my own strength

I too shall firmly endure and live on.

금오산·1 – 채미정 –

금오산 바람결 출렁이는 파도 가슴
하늘 우러러보니
시린 달빛 바람 가득한데!

황혼의 둥지
숨죽이고 눈치만 보네.

채미정에 이르러
야은 선생 보니
당신 가슴 고요히 서있고
바람만 부네.

Mount Geumosan • 1 — Chaemijeong —

In Geumosan's breeze waves stir in my heart

Lifting my gaze to the sky

Chilly moonlit wind is brimming there!

The nest of twilight

Holds its breath watching in silence.

Reaching Chaemijeong

I see Master Yaeun

His heart stands in stillness and

Only the wind blows.

금오산·2 - 호숫가 -

산등성이 휜 골짜기 숨결 끌어안고
쉼 없이 오른다.

금오산, 깊은 영혼 속 천년의 쉼터
가을 하늘빛 꽃바람으로 익은 열매
불꽃으로 피어나고!

저녁노을 물결 춤출 때 낙엽 밟으며
호숫가에 앉아 금오산자락
휘파람으로 노래 부른다.

Mount Geumosan • 2 − By the Lakeside −

Embracing the ridge-curved valleys' breath

I climb without rest.

Geumosan a thousand-year haven deep in the soul

The fruits ripened by the autumn sky's bloomy winds

Bursting forth in flame!

When sunset waves begin to dance

I tread on fallen leaves by the lakeside

Whistling a song to Geumosan's foothills.

금오산·3 – 올레길 –

유월의 바람결 따라
나무 잎새들 은은히
고운 여인의 손길로
피아노 치고 있다.

바람 불어와
내 마음 싣고
금오산 호숫가에 와
올레길 돌고 돌아
금오산 자락 부여잡고

향기에 취해
달빛 바람 맞으며
속삭인다.

Mount Geumosan • 3 – Olle Trail –

Following the June breeze
Leaves of trees' softly rustle
As if a gentle woman's fingers
Playing the piano.

The wind arrives
Carrying my heart
To Geumosan's lakeside
Wandering round the Olle trail
Clinging to its mountain skirts

Drunk on fragrance
Meeting the moonlit wind
I whisper.

4부

신선놀음
A Divine Amusement

물안개 • 1

새벽 아침 길
목욕탕 속같이 희뿌옇다.

초롱초롱 밤부터 새벽이슬
먹고 핀 길가의 꽃들!

아지랑이 아른아른
물안개 피어오른 거리마다

새벽이슬 먹으며 젖어있다.

뿌연 안갯속 아침을 맞는다.

Mist • 1

The road at dawn

Hazy like a bathroom filled with steam.

Roadside flowers drink in the morning dew

Fallen from the sky of sparkling stars!

Shimmering haze wavering gently

Mist rises on every street

Soaked in the morning dew.

I greet the day in the fog's embrace.

물안개 • 2

안개는 피어서
강으로 가고

어느새 펑퍼짐한 허리는
풀어헤쳐진
봄바람 여인처럼
어둡고 칙칙하다.

봄 안개 물 오르면
야릇한 무지개처럼
그윽하다.

Mist • 2

The mist blooms
Then drifts down to the river

Soon its loosened wide hips
Spilled open
Like a woman flushed
With a touch of spring fever
Dim and dusky.

When spring mist brushes
The water deepens subtle
As a shimmering suggestive rainbow.

연꽃 차

볼 연지에 연꽃 한 송이

끌어안고 오므린 잎

마른 잎 제 마음처럼

활짝 펼쳐 속으로

속으로만 우러난다.

Lotus Tea

A single lotus on blushing cheeks

Held close in cupped leaves

Dry leaves like its own heart

Bloom wide open inward

Infusing only from within.

자화상

오만가지 빛깔의 감정으로

갖은 고뇌와 정성, 감동에

춤추는 봄바람, 장맛비

단풍빛 낙엽, 겨울 눈꽃 송이

가슴 밭에 함께 내린다.

자화상

Self-Portrait

With myriad hues of emotion

Carried by anguish, devotion and moving feeling

Spring breezes dancing, summer rains

Tinted autumn leaves, winter snow blossoms

All fall together upon the field of my heart.

석류 • 1

가랑가랑 숨결만 붙은

반으로 잘린 위장

질긴 끈 놓지 않는

사랑 끈 줄기로

석류꽃 수놓듯 피어난다.

Pomegranate • 1

Clinging barely to the faint breath

A stomach split in half

Holding fast to a stubborn thread

Like a cord of love unbroken

Pomegranate flowers burst forth like embroidery.

석류 · 2

침묵으로
맺힌 그리움

바람 흔드는
그대 마음 숨결

진실의 무게만큼
안으로 안으로만
삭이다가

겹겹이 터져버린
붉은 가슴!

Pomegranate • 2

Longing sealed
In silence

Your heart's breath
Stirring the wind

As heavy as the truth
Pressed inward inward until
Consumed within

Until it bursts in layers
A crimson heart!

그리움•3

봄 햇살에 겨우내 움츠렸던 가슴
핑크빛 봄 꽃잎

피어나는 봄바람 눈썹
살랑대며 윙크하는 애교에!

세월의 강(江) 흐르는 소리
흰 구름 떠가는 포근함에

산봉우리 마디마디
희망으로 가득 차올라

아름다운 그리움 자락
끝이 없구나.

Longing • 3

The heart that shrank all winter long

Glows like pink blossoms in the spring sun

Spring breezes lift their eyelashes

Fluttering with a playful wink!

The sound of river of time flowing

White clouds drift in gentle warmth

Each mountain ridge

Swells with hope

The sweep of beautiful longing

Has no end.

가을 산

가을 산이 한층 무르익으며
황금빛으로 익어갈 때

사색하는 가을 산은
노을자락 부여잡고

잃어버린 것과
지나온 발자취를
헤아려본다

이제 다가올 겨울 동안
다소곳이 희망을 꿈꾸며

가져야할 것을
다짐하며

새 봄을 맞이할 것이다.

Autumn Mountain

As the autumn mountain ripens deeper, and

Turns to shades of gold

The autumn mountain in meditation

Clings to the trailing hem of the sunset

Reflecting on

What was lost and

The footsteps left behind

Through the winter soon to come

It will quietly dream of hope

Resolving

To carry what must be taken

I will welcome the new spring.

귀가

싸늘한 네온사인이
울고 있는 밤

돌아가자
따뜻한 눈물
가슴 열고

시간의 강(江)을 건너
어디든 가자

부대끼며 허우적대며
건너서 가자

사랑도
눈물도
아픔도
그리움도
모두 다 가자

싸늘한 바람이 꿈꾼다
우리 가야 할
문 하나 열린
그곳으로 가자.

Homecoming

In the night
When the cold neon signs weep

Let us return
With warm tears
Opening our hearts

Crossing the river of time
Let us go anywhere

Pushed, struggling
Let us cross and go

Love and
Tears and
Pain and
Longing
Let us take them all

Bleak wind dreams

Of the place we must go

Through a single open door

Let us go.

동백이 눈뜨는 날

늦가을 지는 햇살에 빈 가슴을 적실 때
갈대는 빛을 잃고 억새가 숨죽이고
쓸쓸한 밤을 시린 듯 운다

한겨울 해안 절벽
하얀 눈 어둠 밝히며 등대로 서는

동백이 눈뜨는 날은
뜨겁게 붉어온다.

When Camellias Open Their Eyes

When the fading late autumn's light soaks my heart

Reeds fade Silver grasses hold their breath

And in the lonely nights they weep as if chilled

On the midwinter coastal cliffs

Standing like a lighthouse snow-lit darkness

When camellias open their eyes

The day rises burning red.

달

하늘 바다에 외로이 선다
달빛은 그리움의 발자국
따라가고 있다

그대의 보드라운 숨결로
눈물 닦으며
구름 즈려밟고

고개 저편 언덕으로부터
살그머니 사라지고
나도 달빛 따라 흘러갑니다.

Moon

Standing alone on the sea of sky

Moonlight follows

The footprints of longing

With your tender breath

Wiping away tears

Stepping softly on the clouds

Beyond the hill far

Quietly slips away and

I too drift on following the moonlight.

세상 기슭

세월의 강(江)은
흐르고 흘러
스스로 쌓이고 쌓였던
마음 자락 큰 산 되어

그 산기슭에 앉아
둘러보니
사방팔방
피어나는 꽃들

피고 지고
다시 태어나는
향기로운 세상!

Edge of the World

The river of time

Flows and flows

Piling upon itself

Becoming a mountain formed in my heart

Sitting at its foot

I look around

And everywhere

Flowers are blooming

Blooming, fading,

Born anew again

This fragrant world!

네가 가던 그날은

네가 가던 그날은
하늘이 슬피 울고
참새도 울고
나도 울었다.

온통 울음바다
그치질 않고
봄 끝자락 마디마디 울어서
퉁퉁 부어 있었다.

네가 가던 그날의 눈물이
너무 젖어
압록강, 한강, 낙동강
빨갛게 타오르며
철철 넘쳐흘렀다.

The Day You Left

The day you left

The sky wept bitterly

Sparrows wept

And I wept too.

Until the world

Became a sea of sorrow

Even the spring's last edge

Every joint

Swollen with tears.

Drenched too deeply

In the tears of the day you left

The Amnok, the Han, the Nakdong

Burned red and

Overflowed in torrents.

혼자 우는 바다

바람이 분다

서글픈 바다는 파도가 되어

목메어 울어대니

갈매기도 운다

그리움에

수평선 너머 붉게 타는

황혼도 운다.

Sea Weeping Alone

The wind blows

The sorrowful sea becomes waves

Choking with cries

Even the seagulls weep

In longing

The burning red dusk weeps as well

Beyond the horizon.

신선놀음

하늘에선 단풍잎 하나
맑은 약수 한잔 마시며
시 한수 읊으니
참새도 함께 노래한다

해 질 녘 가을꽃자리에
길게 돗자리 펴고
드러누워

앞으로는 계곡물
소곤소곤 속삭이며 흐르고
뒤로는 울창한 숲
그늘 드리우니
맑고도 그윽하기 한이 없다.

A Divine Amusement

In the sky one autumn leaf sways

I drink a cup of clear spring water

And recite a poem

Even sparrows join the song

At dusk among the autumn blossoms

I spread a long mat

And lie back

Before me the valley stream

Whispers softly as it flows

Behind me the dense forest

Casts its shade

Pure and profound without end.

시인의 꿈

갈대밭 밑그림 치며
둥글게 수채화를 그릴 때

소쩍새 울음소리
불새도 기웃거리며
도도한 가을 여인의 자태

봄 그리고 가을 목련꽃
피고 지고 가슴 열고
당신과 다짐할 때
비로소 시인이 되어
사랑의 꽃 붉게 피우리라.

A Poet's Dream

On the sketch of a reed field

When I paint in soft rounded watercolors

The cry of a Scops-owl

And even the Firebird is drawn near

By the stately figure of an Autumn Woman

When spring and autumn Magnolias

Bloom and fall hearts open wide

And in vows with you

I at last become a poet

Letting the flower of love blaze in red.

연인

당신을 만났던 어제의 길
당신과 함께 갈 수 없는 길
당신과 희로애락을
노래하는 내일이 있는 길

하늘께서 주신 행복의 시간(時間)
노을 짓는 하늘 바닷가 끝이라도

월 화 수 목 금 토 일
늘 한결같이 지금처럼만
사랑한다는 것에 만족하며

흐르는 강(江)처럼
당신과 나
참으로 행복 합니다.

Lovers

The path of yesterday where I first met you

The path I cannot walk with you and

The path of tomorrow

Singing of joy and sorrow with you

The blessed time Heaven has given

Even at the far edge of sea and sunset sky

Mon Tue Wed Thu Fri Sat and Sunday

Always the same just as now

Content in love

Like a river flowing

You and I

Are truly happy.

생명 • 1

내 아직 못 다한 꿈이 있기에
예전엔 가지 못하고
먼 숲의 나무가 되었지만

가까이 오리
아빠의 가슴처럼
깃털을 달고
따뜻한 불꽃이 되어

줄기세포마다 일란성 쌍둥이
욕심쟁이 두 돌 박이 자매
생명의 봄이 오리라.

Life • 1

Because of the dreams not yet fulfilled

In the past I could not go and

Became a tree in a distant forest

Yet I will come near

With feathers like Daddy's chest

Becoming a warm flame

Every stem cell identical twins

Greedy two years old twin sisters

The spring of life will come.

5부

숨어 우는 바람 소리에
The Weeping Wind In Hiding

시인의 마음

시어가 온통 머릿속을 맴돌다
벽과 천장에 돋아난다

귀를 막고 눈을 감아도
자꾸만 떠올라
새벽부터 머리 감고
목욕하고 냉수를 마셔도

천장에서 내려오는
시어 때문에
삼복더위조차도 잊고
마음대로 써 내려간다.

The Poet's Heart

Poetic words circle all through my mind

Then sprout on the walls and ceiling

Even when I cover my ears and close my eyes

They keep returning

Even from dawn when I wash my hair

Bathe and drink cold water

Because of those poetic words

Falling from the ceiling

I forget even the midsummer heat and

Write without restraint.

바람 부는 날

바람은 자꾸만 손짓하며
이야기하잖다

하얀 목련꽃처럼
홀로 가야할 외로움

하늘을 쳐다보아도
알 수 없는 그리움의 꽃

내 가슴의 향기로운
꽃 잎새 바람에 밀려와

굽이치는 추억의 소리
휘청거리는 봄!

A Windy Day

The wind keeps gesturing

As if want to talk

Like a White Magnolia blossom

In loneliness I must walk alone

Even when I look to the sky

A flower of yearning I cannot name

The fragrant petals drift into my heart

Carried on the wind

The sounds of surging memories

Wavering spring!

초승달•1

초승달 기울어 가고
저 별은 그대별
내 별은 기울고 못생긴
초승달 옆 조그마한 별!

별빛 따라
바람 따라
흘러가는 나그네 별

초승달 그만 기울고
내 별빛 따라
같이 흐르자.

Crescent Moon • 1

As the crescent new moon tilts away

That star is your star

My star is the tiny star

Beside the crooked crescent moon!

Following the starlight

Following the wind

A wandering star drifts along

Crescent, no longer fade, and

Follow my starlight and

Let us drift together.

초승달 · 2

초승달 별빛
호수에 빠져 있다.

건져내어
내 마음 거울로 삼고

앵두나무 가지 위에
꽃으로 피고 흐른다.

Crescent Moon • 2

The crescent and starlight

Are drowned in the lake.

Fishing them out

I make them the mirror of my heart

Upon the cherry tree branches

It blooms as flowers and flows away.

오월의 철쭉

말없이 봄은 차례로 가고

동백꽃도 가고

벚꽃, 목련꽃도

가버렸으나

오월의 핑크빛 철쭉은

아름답고 고운 꽃구름으로

뭉게뭉게 피어났다.

Pink Azaleas of May

Silently spring passes in turn

Camellias fade

Cherry blossoms and magnolias too

All have slipped away

But the pink azaleas of May

Rise like clouds of blossoms

Billowing, blooming in fullness.

그 한 사람

남 어려움에 안타까워
눈물 고인 가슴
꽃보다 아름답다

어떤 꽃인들
아름답지 않은
꽃은 없다

여유로움
나누어 주는
꽃처럼 아름다운

그 한 사람이
무척 아름답다.

That One Person

Moved with sorrow for another's hardship

The heart brimming with tears

More beautiful than any flower

For is there no flower

That is not beautiful

In its own way

Like a flower

That shares its grace

And gives abundance

That one person

Is truly beautiful.

꽃과 물

나무는 시인이 되어
가지 끝으로 말하고

꽃은
꽃을 좋아하는
그리운 사람에게 말하고

물은
압록강에서도
한강에서도
낙동강에서도
끊임없이 흐르며 말한다.

Flowers And Water

The tree becomes a poet

Speaking through the tips of its branches

The flower

Speaks to the beloved one

Who loves flowers

The water

In the Amnok River

In the Han River

In the Nakdong River

Speaks in its endless flowing.

숨어 우는 바람 소리에•1

시간의 강(江)을 뛰어넘은 바람 소리에
무지개 떠다니고
내 마음의 바다엔 큰 배가 떠다닙니다.

하지만 하늘 호숫가 가로지른 구름은
훨씬 예쁘게 춤을 추며 가고

당신과 나와의 만남
며칠 밤 지새워 가슴 열어 젖혀
꽃을 피우고

선녀와 나무꾼처럼 한결같은 일상의
투명한 호흡으로 단풍길 숲속 저편에서
숨어 우는 바람 소리에

흔들리는 갈대의 속삭임 되어
함박꽃 웃음의 청춘 바람 불어옵니다.

숨어 우는 바람 소리에•1

The Weeping Wind In Hiding • 1

In the sound of the wind over the river of time

A rainbow drifts and

In the sea of my heart a great ship sails.

Yet the clouds crossing the lakeside sky

Dance past with far greater beauty

Meeting of you and I

Kept us awake for nights until our hearts opened

And bloomed like flowers

Like the story of the Woodcutter and the Heavenly Maiden

With the steady breath of everyday life

Beyond the autumn-tinted forest path

In the sound of the winds weeping in hiding

Becoming the whisper of swaying reeds

And a wind of youthful laughter blows bright.

숨어 우는 바람 소리에 • 2

당신 모습 아른거려 숨어 우는 바람 소리에
기억의 꽃들 겨울 나목 되어 질긴 인생
당당하고 끈끈한 인연으로 맺은 생명 꽃 인생!

노란 꽃잎 피고 지고 푸른 잎 되고
단풍 지고 낙엽 밟으며 외로워질 때
기인 바람 불어와 그리움은 떠나가고

동지섣달 눈보라 필 때
빨갛게 익어가는 눈보라 웃음
감동 꽃으로 살아가리라.

The Weeping Wind In Hiding • 2

In the sound of the weeping wind in hiding

Your image shimmers as memory's flowers turn to winter trees

Life endures the flower of resilience bound in steadfast ties!

Yellow petals bloom and fall, turning into green leaves

Walking among the autumn leaves my loneliness deepens

One long strand of wind rises and longing drifts away

When the midwinter blizzard blows

With laughter ripening red like snowflakes

I will live as a moving flower.

송년의 노래

나의 노래는 알몸으로 뒤집혀
강(江)에 떠가고 있다

꺾인 나뭇가지에 핀
기억의 꽃들이
어둠 속에서 나의 얼굴이 되어
이지러진 꿈의 벼랑을 타오르고 있다

어둠을 분해하는 수줍은 꿈 조각
허리 꺾인 깊은 시간 속에
찬연(粲然)한 아침은 일어서고 있다

경건한 빛살을 건져 올리며
투명한 알몸으로 바람을 어루만진다.

송년의 노래

Song of the Year's End

My song laid bare drifts

Upside down upon the river

On the broken branches

Bloom the flowers of memories

In the darkness they become my face

Climbing the cliff of a waning dream

Shy fragments of dream dissolve the darkness

From the bent waist of deep time

Brilliant morning stands

Lifting solemn rays of light

With a transparent body it caresses the wind.

아스팔트가의 단풍나무들

고통을 껴안고 묵묵히 미소로 서 있는
마지막 가는 시월의 아스팔트 위에
질책이라도 하듯
활활 타오르는 나의 젊음도
이제는 갈 길을 잃어
여기저기 나뒹굴고 있소.

머얼리서 울리는 기적 소리도
한 차례 깊은 바람도
정녕 아쉬움으로
뜨거움을 남기며
옷깃을 여미고 있소.

나는 바람과 바람 사이를
헤집고 다니며
생명을 불어넣고 있소.

불끈 솟아오른 빌딩 숲 사이로도
가을은 날갯짓하며
퍼덕이고 있소.

생명은 찬란한 단풍빛으로
채색(彩色)되어 영겁(永劫)의 날들을
영롱한 진실로 맞아들이고 있소.

그 어디메이뇨
황혼이 짙어갈 즈음
마음을 비우고
비로소 가슴을 열며
황금빛 생명의 불 위를 걷는
신비의 여인이 되겠소.

아픔을 딛고 피어나는
숙명의 꽃이기에
기다리고 기다리고
또 기다리겠소.

다시 태어날 그 날들을…….

Maple Trees on the Asphalt Road

Embracing pain standing silently with a smile

On the asphalt of late October

As if in reproach

Even my burning youth

Now has lost its way

Scattered here and there.

The train's cry far away

A deep wind sweeping through

Leaving behind

Trace of warmth

Tighten their collars.

Between one wind to another

I wander stirring

Breathing life into the air.

Even through the forest of rising buildings

Autumn spreads its wings

And flutters.

Maple Trees on the Asphalt Road

Life is dyed in brilliant autumn hues

Welcoming the endless days

With radiant truth.

And somewhere

As twilight thickens

I will empty my heart

Open my bosom at last

To walk upon the golden fire of life

A woman of mystery.

For I fated a flower

Blooming upon pain

I will wait again, and again

And again.

For the day to be born again······.

동백꽃 •1

시린 가슴 설렘도

하염없이 타오르는 겨울 꽃

끝내 뻐꾸기 사랑처럼

둥지를 틀어

인내, 희생, 용서, 기쁨

감사의 꽃을 피우는구나!

Camellia · 1

A trembling heart in the cold

An endlessly burning winter flower

At last like a cuckoo's fleeting love

Building its nest

Blossoming into flowers of

Patience, Sacrifice, Forgiveness, Joy

And Gratitude!

동백꽃·2

겨울부터 추위에도 은근히
빨갛게 피기 시작해서
삼월의 지금까지 피우고 있는

너의 생명 조금씩
빛바래고 있다
어쩌겠니
하늘이 주신 운명인 걸!

피었다 지고
다시 피는 새 생명
열릴 때까지 기다려야지.

Camellia • 2

From the winter's cold

Quietly began to bloom red and

Still in March you bloom

Your life little by little

Fades of colors

But what can be done

It is the destiny given by heaven!

Blooming fading

Blooming once more

Until new life opens you wait.

동백꽃·3

빨갛고 예쁜 모습 떠나보내고

황혼길 숲속 같은 마음 숨결

여유로이 날개 펼쳐

행복 신고서

하늘 꽃밭으로 날으오리다.

Camellia • 3

Sending away your red and lovely face

Like breath in a twilight forest path

With ease you spread your wings

Carrying happiness

You will soar to heaven's flower fields.

동백꽃•4 – 생강나무 –

여기저기서 들리는 생명들의 숨결
산기슭에서 상냥한 겨울 여인! 동백꽃
빨갛고 아름답게 활짝 핀다.

초록빛 무명치마 산허리 휘어 감고
산 넘고 강(江) 건너 붉게 피어나는 소리가 들린다.

생강나무 노오란 등불 인내하는 오솔길
이젠 머지않아 아카시아꽃 하늘 아래
향기 품어 온 산에 벌, 나비 불러 모아

내가 좋아하는 사람들께
산 향기와 봄 향기를 아낌없이 주고 싶어
겨울부터 봄까지 미소 짓는 아름다운
그대 동백꽃!

Everywhere the breath of life is heard

On the mountain slope a gentle Winter Lady! Camellia

Red and radiant, you bloom wide.

A green cotton skirt wraps the mountain's waist

Over hills and rivers red blossoms resound.

On the path Spicebush endures with yellow lanterns lit

Soon Acacias will cover the sky with flowers

Fragrance fills the mountain, calling bees and butterflies

To those you love

To give freely the fragrance of mountain and spring

Smiling from winter into spring

Beautiful Camellia You Radiant One!

님이시여, 때가 왔습니다

지난봄부터 아픔이 오고
삶의 지혜가 필요했던 만큼
고뇌와 인내를 배우며
살아왔습니다.

고장 난 시계처럼 고치고 수리하며
아낌없이 구구절절이
사랑을 배웠습니다.

이제는 때가 왔습니다.

해결되지 않은 모든 문제에 대해
온몸으로 부딪히며
살아야 되리라는 것을
이제야 깨달았습니다.

조급하게 찾기보다
기도하며 기다리면
알찬 열매가 열린다는 것을!

문제 그 자체를 사랑하며
경험한다는 것은
행복이란 것을!

그러면 먼 훗날 자신도 모르게
기쁨이 온다는 것을!

아픔이 있기에 성장하고
참으로 행복이란 것을
알았습니다.

Beloved, the Time Has Come

Since last spring pain has come and
As much as I needed the wisdom of life
I have lived
Learning anguish and patience.

Like a broken clock mended and repaired
Without holding back in every detail
I have learned love.

Now the time has come.

For every unresolved problem
I have realized at last
That I must face it
With my whole being.

Rather than seeking in haste
If I pray and wait
I will see fruitful harvests!

To love the problem itself

To experience it

Is to know happiness!

And then in a far-off tomorrow

Without knowing how joy will come!

Because there is pain there is growth

And I have come to know

That this truly is happiness.

봄빛 건배 잔

봄은 빗속에 핑크빛 들어
건배하듯

나도 내 마음의 잔을 들어
건배합니다

담기는 건 고통뿐일지언정
내 마음은 어여쁜 잔이 될 것입니다

담기는 빗방울 마디마디
꽃과 잎은 빗속에 물들이고 있습니다

생기 없는 슬픔에 담긴 젖은 술은
생생한 황금의 들녘처럼
빛바랬습니다

그래도 내 마음의 빈 잔은
화기애애한 당신의 포도주가
되리라는 것을
믿어 의심치 않습니다.

Toasting Glass of Spring Light

As spring holds a pink glow in the rain
Raising a toast

I too lift the glass of my heart and
Offer my own

Though what it holds may be only pain
My heart will be a lovely glass

Every gathered raindrop
Is tinted by flowers and leaves

The wine steeped in lifeless grief
Has faded
Like golden fields once vivid

And yet still my empty heart's glass
I trust without doubt
Will be filled
With your radiant wine.

당신 앞에선

그리움 때문에
행복한 눈물의 가슴

할 이야기가
하늘만큼 많은데

당신 앞에선 맑은 눈망울이
벙어리 냉가슴이
되어 버려요

두근두근
눈물 고인 내 가슴

알면서도
모르는 척
시침 떼는 여유

날 바라봐요 가슴속
언어들의 응어리를
보듬어 주세요.

Before You

Because of longing
My heart brims with happy tears

I have stories left to share
As boundless as the sky

Before you
Even my clear bright gaze
Becomes a silent frozen heart

Thump thump
My chest fills with tears

You know
Yet pretend not to know
With your quiet detachment

Look at me please
Embrace the tangled words
Knotted in my heart.

보낼 수 없는 그대

내 마음 흔들릴 때는
차마 마주 보지 못해

하늘 올려다보며
큰 숨을 쉬다가
눈을 감는다

그렇다고 어여쁜
그대 길 잃고
헤맬까 봐

아예 외면하고
눈 감을 수도 없어
내가 먼저 그대에게
손을 내민다

영롱한 사랑이여
나를 잊지 말아주오.

The One I Cannot Let Go

When my heart is shaken and
Cannot bear to face you

I lift my eyes to the sky
Breathe deeply and
Close them

Yet I fear my fair beloved
Might lose the path and
Wander away

Yet I cannot turn aside
Nor keep my eyes closed
Instead I reach out
My hand to you first

O radiant love
Please Do Not Forget me.

지난날은 별이 되었다

지나간 하루하루를

불꽃이 태웠다

시간을 태워서

재가 되어

내려앉은

지난날의 죽은 과거가

별이 되어 흔적으로 탄생되었다.

Bygone Days Become Stars

I burned

Each passing day

Burning time itself

Until it turned to ashes and

Scattered to the ground

The dead past of the days gone by

Has been born as a star

As a relic.

속삭임

꽃을 흔들고 가는 바람 속으로
하늘의 소리가 들려온다.

졸고 있는 길목을, 흔들어 깨우면
별들의 이야기가 들려온다.

별 하나의 은은한 절규와
꽃 하나마다 피는 횃불의 즙

"그림자여, 그림자여"
오, 나르는 사고(思考)의 머플러여!

휘파람을 부세요!

그러면
날개를 활짝 펼쳐
한껏 날 거예요.

모든 허상 뿌리치고
감성과 이성의 가지마다 헤쳐

능선을 타고 유유히 흘러가는
가을 하늘처럼

조금은 따사롭고 조금은 서늘한 연인으로
당신께 다가갈 거예요.

"저어 휘파람을 부세요, 네?"

그러면
긴 날개 몸부림으로
둥지를 틀어

천지(天地)간 바람 되어
산천초목(山川草木)을 쓸며

한 점 부끄러움 없는
태초의 모습 그대로

파르르 열린 가슴으로
가을 햇살 한 아름 피울거예요.

Whisper

Into the passing wind stirring the flowers
Comes the sound of the sky.

When drowsy crossroads are shaken awake
The stories of the stars are heard.

The gentle cry of a single star
Torchlike sap blooming in every flower

"Shadow, O shadow"
Oh muffler of flying thought!

Give a whistle!

Then
I will spread my wings wide and
Fly with all my might.

Shedding all illusions
Cutting through feelings and reasons

Like the autumn sky
Drifting freely along the ridgeline

As a lover a little warm, a little cool
I will draw near to you.

"Please whistle on, won't you?"

Then
With the long struggle of wings
I will build my nest

Becoming the wind of heaven and earth
Brushing mountains streams and fields

With not a single trace of shame
In the very form of the beginning

With a trembling yet open heart
I will bloom an armful of autumn light.

나의 문학관

시향 권영주

현대문학이란? 즉, 인생의 가치와 철학을 환희의 웃음과 감동의 눈물로 자아낸다. 시적자아를 지닌 사람 즉, 시를 쓰고 읽어야하는 시인들과 독자들의 영혼이 꽃을 보듯 꽃 앞에서 인생의 깊은 의미를 보듯 열렬히 호소하는 것을 알아야 되고 청초한 소녀의 자아, 시인의 삶의 간이역에 즐거움과 희망, 기쁨, 행복, 소망만 있는 건 아니기에 시대의 아픔과 시간의 희로애락을 느끼며 삶을 살아가고 인생의 파노라마처럼 담대히 받아들이려고 애쓰며 시인은 다양한 표현을 하고 싶어 한다.

그러므로 모든 걸 쏟아낸다. 시간 시간을 아까워하고 반기면서 만끽한다. 몰래 사색의 뜰에서 깊이 울기도 하고 웃기도 하면서 삶이란 인생 속에서 마치 깊이 길어 올려 마시는 생명수처럼 절실하고 활기찬 회복을 느낀다.

이 같은 아포리즘 성격의 시편을 대할 수 있는 것은 참으로 행복하다. 이윽고, 사랑을 느끼고 가치를 공유하는 기회가 된다는 것은 참으로 감사한 일입니다.

시인은 아름다움을 볼 줄 아는 지혜가 있어야 하고 소중한 감성을 느껴야 하고 순수 그 자체의 진리를 알아야 하고 삶의 꽃을 피울 줄 아는 영혼의 맑은 눈이 필요 합니다.

My Poetic Vision

Sihyang Kwon Young-Joo

What is modern literature? It reaveals life's values and philosophy through radiant laughter and moving tears. Those with a poetic soul, the poets who write and the readers who read, see in a flower the deeper meaning of life, hearing its silent appeals and glimpsing the innocence of a maiden's spirit. A poet's path holds not only joy and hope but also the sorrows of the age and the shifting emotions of existence, embraced with courage and given expression.

Thus, everything is poured out. Each moment is treasured, welcomed, and savored. In the garden of reflection, one may quietly weep or laugh, yet within life itself, like drawing up and drinking living water, one finds renewal, urgency, and vitality. To encounter such aphoristic verses is a blessing, and to feel love and share its worth is a gift beyond measure.

A poet must have the wisdom to perceive beauty, the sensitivity to cherish it, the purity to know the truth, and the clear eyes of the soul to bring life's flowers into bloom.

문학과 철학

시향 권영주

인간은 생존을 결정해 가는 실존이며 이유 없이 태어나서 이유 없이 던져진 자기를 받아 주는 자신인 것이다. 부조리의 정신은 허위에 몸을 맡기는 것보다는 즉, 절망을 두려움 없이 선택하는 게 더욱 현명할 것이다. 오늘날 인간은 전체에서 분리되고 고립되어 자기 혼자의 힘으로 돌아가게 되고 그와는 공통한 것이라곤 하나도 없고 또한 이때 운명의 얼굴을 가진 현실이 둘러싸고 있는 것을 발견한다.

우리의 문학은 인간과 세계의 관계를 생각하고 상상하고 느끼기 위한 도구가 아니다. 우리의 행위의 형이상학적이며 도덕적인 울림에 대한 것이다. 또한 우리의 운명에 대한 것이다. 오늘날의 문학은 아주 조그마한 사실이나 삽화의 문맥 그 자체를 묻는 것이다. 즉, 살아가는 문제와 왜 살아야 하는가를 묻는 것이다. 문학은 곧 예술이요 예술의 가치는 미가 아니고 엄격한 요구와 순결인 것이다.

사르트르의 말처럼 인간은 자유이며 인생은 절망의 이면(裏面)에서 시작된다고 한다. 모든 미의 깊숙한 곳에서는 무엇인가 비인간적인 것이 가로놓여 있다. 인간의 가장 깊은 곳으로 호소하려는 욕망에 직면으로 태도를 취할 때 비합리적인 것이 나타나는 것이다. 정신의 욕망과 이를 받아들이려는 세계와의 이반(離反)과 나의 동경(憧憬)과 해체(解體)한 우주와 이것들을 싸돌고 있는 모순의 실을 절망의 벼랑 위에선 인간이 보는 것이다. 문명이 한계를 만들어 위협하며 포위하고 있다는 것을 인간은 알아야 한다. 인간성이나 인격은 절대로 도달할 수 없는 하나의 과제요 가능성이리라. 혹은 환영(幻影)일지도 모른다. 그럼에도 불구하고 그 실현을 목표로 하지 않을 수도 없는 것이다.

　문학은 곧 예술이요 정신과 이성에 의한 생활 비평이다. 정신은 생활을 비평하고 해부하여 용서 없는 메스를 넣는다. 생활을 발가벗겨 거꾸로 하고 집어 던지고 난도질을 한다. 그리하여 그것을 베껴 쓰는 것에 의하여 심판한다. '작가나 비평가가 써서 구원 된다'라고 말하는 것이다. 살아 있지 않는 것은 만들 수가 없으며, 사랑하지 않는 것은 알 수가 없다. 작가는 살아있어야 하고 실존하여야 한다. 현대의 작가의 운명은 실로 비극적이리라. 결코 도달할 수 없는 과제를 향해 시지프스와 같은 노력을 계속한다. 도달 했다고 생각하면 환각(幻覺)에 불과했다는 것이 판명되어 또다시 원래의 상태로 되돌아온다. 그래도 거기에서 포기할 수는 없다. 플라톤은 '철학이란 혼의 파닥거림이다'라고 했다. 작가가 자기의 작품 속에서 혼의 날개의 파닥거림을 따라서 철학을 느낄 때 그 작품은 위대한 작품이 될 것이요. 그때 작가는 위대한 통찰의 순간을 가질 것이다. 철학과 문학의 경계가 이때 자유로이 용해되고 철학이 문학 속에 녹아 들어가서 인간의 정신을 황홀하게 할 것이다.

Literature and Philosophy

Sihyang Kwon Young-Joo

Human beings are existence itself, thrown into life without reason, and must accept the self that has been cast into the world. To surrender to falsehood, the spirit of absurdity, is less wise than to choose despair without fear. Today, humanity finds itself separated and isolated, forced to rely on its own strength, discovering that with others it shares little in common. At such a moment, reality appears with the face of fate.

Our literature is not merely a tool to think, imagine, or feel the relation between human and the world, but a resonance of metaphysical and moral actions. It is also bound to destiny. The contemporary literature questions the smallest of facts or fragments, yet at its core it asks the central questions: how we live, and why we must live. Literature is an art, and the value of art lies not in beauty but in its stern demands and purity.

As Sartre said, man is freedom, and life begins in the shadow of despair. At the depth of all beauty lies something inhuman. When we confront the deepest longing of the human spirit, the irrational emerges. Humanity stands at the edge of despair, perceiving both the desire of the spirit and the estrangement of the world, longing for the universe broken apart yet bound by threads of contradiction. A civilization builds its own limits, threatening and enclosing us. A personhood itself may be an unattainable task, perhaps only an illusion, yet the one we cannot refuse to pursue.

Literature is an art, but also a critique of life by mind and reason. The spirit dissects and judges, laying a bare existence, stripping it down, reversing it, casting it aside. In rewriting it, the writer becomes a judge. "The writer or critic is saved by what is written," it is said. What is not alive cannot create, and what is not loved cannot be known. The writer must live and exist. The fate of the modern writer is indeed tragic, doomed to a Sisyphean struggle toward an unattainable task. To believe one has reached it only to realize it was an illusion, then has to begin again. Yet surrender is impossible. Plato said, "Philosophy is the fluttering of the soul." When a writer feels in his work the flutter of wings of the soul, then the work becomes great, and the writer experiences a moment of true insight. At such a point, the boundary between philosophy and literature dissolves, and philosophy within literature enchants the human spirit.

서평
Commentary

마침내 꽃이 되다

새로운 언어의 차원으로 내면의 힘,
영혼의 아름다움을 건축하다.

이철호(소설가, 문학평론가)

언어는 그 사람을 표상한다. 언어가 곧 그 사람인 줄도 모른다. 사람은 언어를 통하여 사고(思考)하고 소통하기에, 언어에는 그 사람의 어떠함이 담기기 마련이다. 반대로 언어는 사람을 만들어 간다. 역시 언어를 통해 사고하기 때문이다. 생각은 반드시 삶의 어떤 영역에서든 반영되고 드러난다. 언어는 보이지 않는 것 같지만 분명한 세계를 가지고, 개인이든, 사회든 가치를 형성한다. 윤석열 대통령의 계엄으로, 다른 때보다 많이 쓰였던 단어는 '프레임'이었다.(정치는 어찌 보면 프레임 전쟁이라고 한다.) 이때의 프레임은 형틀 같은 느낌이다.

왜 난데없이 정치 이야기며 프레임 이야기를 하냐고? 그렇듯 언어는 감옥이 되기도 하고 '진리를 알지니 진리가 너희를 자유케 하리라(요한복음 8:32)'는 '자유'의 날개로 기능하기 때문이다.

권영주 시인은 언어의 차원을 새롭게 해석하고 적용하는 데 천재적이다.

즉 개개 언어가 갖고 있는 인식을 뒤엎는 실험적 시도가 그의 시에서는 완성도 높게 안착하여 놀랍도록 아름다운 형상화를 이룬다. 단지 언어적 경계를 허문 이미지화의 성공만이 아니라 인간 본연의 정서가 산들바람처럼 불어와 시의 편편이 극치의 예술성을 보여주는 것이다.

하지만 더욱 그의 시의 완성도를 높이는 것은 삶의 태도와 연관된 내면의 힘이다. 사실 인격의 성숙을 가장 귀한 가치로 여기는 것은 의아스런 일이다. 고매함이거나 우아함 따위가 고물 취급을 받는 시대를 감안한다면 말이다. 하지만 시인은 세상의 눈에 흔들리지 않는다. 오로지 가야 할 길을 가는 길에서 만나는 삶의 아름다움을 온전히 누릴 뿐이다. 시집 『물 향기 수목원』은 강하고 견고한 내면의 힘을 보여주어 '마침내 꽃이 된 여인'의 이야기이다.

먼저 〈물 향기 수목원〉은 깊은 안도감 안에서 그리움 물빛 윤슬로 빛난다. 아득한 옛날부터 켜켜이 쌓아온 그리움이지만 묵은 냄새가 없다. 슬픈 것은 더더욱 아니다. 그 그리움이 오히려 찬연한 이유는 '녹이 슨 거울'을 닦듯 그리움의 창을 열고 그 그리움의 대상과 마주하여 이야기하며 곧잘 기억을 새롭게 하기 때문이다. 그리하여 방금 쪄낸 호빵처럼, 기억은 따끈따끈해진다.

권영주 시인의 시는 정(情)적이다. 하지만 정(情)이란 시어가 내포하고 있을 법한 투박하거나 촌스러움은 찾아볼 수 없다. 엄혹한 시간을 견디고 얼음 속을 뚫고 나온 복수초처럼 그의 정은 반갑고 생기롭다. 마치 첫 생명의 탄생이 간직하고 있는 신비로움과 경외감 같은 것이 그의 시를 견인하고 있는 주된 정서라고 한다면 이 시 〈물 향기 수목원〉이 그렇다.

제목 〈물 향기 수목원〉에서 말하는 '물 향기'는 어떤 것일까? 갯내음

은 아닐 터, 갯벌에서 나무들이 무성히 자라지는 않는다. 그렇다면 온
갖 생물이 유영하는 민물의 비릿하지만 짜지 않는 향기로움일까. 어쨌
든, 생명을 키우는 원시의 물, 퐁퐁 솟아나는 샘의 향기로 상징되고 있
는 것은 분명해 보인다. 수목원은 원래 수목원(樹木園)일테지만 앞의
물 향기에 연원되어 수목원(水木園)으로 이중적으로 육감된다.

모처럼 너를 찾아간 길
고운 햇살에 바람이 곱다.

햇살도 숨을 몰아쉬며
계절의 강을 건넌다.
모처럼 너를 찾아간 길

수양버들 진달래 명자꽃
왼 주머니에 바람을 넣고
오른 주머니에 웃음꽃을
숨겨와

봄볕이 들면 모두 꺼내어
진달래 웃고 있는 그 곳에
산으로 엄마와 진달래 꽃향기를
마시러 간다.

진달래꽃이 가득 배부르면

가슴에 달고 계시는 엄마를
연분홍 꽃잎이 육자배기를
구성지게 불러준다.

엄마는 반짝이는 봄볕에 나와서
갖은 양념으로 버무려 맛있게 무쳐낸다.
봄 햇살 밥과 더불어 한껏 맛이 있었다.

- 〈물 향기 수목원〉

　첫 문장 '모처럼 너를 찾아간 길'이란 평범하면서도 깊은 정을 느끼게 하는 시구이다. 오래도록 마음에 있지만 뜨겁거나 너를 보길 원하는 열망이 급박한 것도 아니다. 잔잔하게 마음 바닥에 깔려 있기에 항상 너를 보는 듯하지만, 그래도 너를 확인해 보자고 하는 마음의 표현이다. '햇살도 숨을 몰아쉬며/ 계절의 강을 건넌다'로 가시화된 '모처럼'은 너를 보지 못한 세월이 길었음을, 숨을 몰아쉬어야 할 만큼 삶이 녹록하지 않았음을 떠올리게 한다. 그럼에도 그것이 비탄이거나 좌절이거나 낙망이 아니었음을 '햇살'을 통해 이미지화하고 있다. 항상 내 마음 안에 있었지만 그만큼 '모처럼'은 너를 보는 '반가움'을 대변하고 있기도 하다. '수양버들 진달래 명자꽃/ 왼 주머니에 바람을 넣고/ 오른 주머니에 웃음꽃을 숨겨와'는 뛰어난 운율감 속에 동화적인 이미지가 보태어져 발랄함, 경쾌함이 신비함의 무게를 옅게 한다. 이는 현실과 상상의 세계를 통합하는 접점으로 기능하고 있다.
　시의 하반부는 봄볕 아래 엄마와 얼마나 따뜻하고 아름다웠던가를

묘사하고 있다. 결국 화자가 '모처럼 너를 찾아간 길'은 엄마와의 추억을 대면하러 가는 길이기도 하다.

어머니가 '반짝이던 봄볕으로 무쳐내었던 반찬과 봄 햇살 밥'이 그리웠으리라. 결국 화자의 강인함은 '따뜻함'이 아닌가 생각되어지는 대목이다. 아무리 추워도 화자의 내면에 있는 사랑과 그 추억의 따뜻한 봄볕이 여전히 온기를 발하고 있어 어려움과 추위를 쉬이 넘길 수 있는 저력이 될 것이다.

이러한 단순한 예는 아마도 〈겨울 산〉이 될 것이다.

바람들이 마디마디 풀어 헤쳐
오늘을 토해내고야 말았다!

돌아온 마음같이
떠나간 너의 마음이여
빛으로 사는 물결

내 가슴에도 성탑을 쌓고
오늘을 보내는
쉰 목소리가 되었다.

있으면 있는 대로
산은 말이 없고
봄, 여름, 가을도 잊고
홀로 불씨 지펴

살아가고 있다.

- 〈겨울 산〉

'바람들이 마디마디/ 풀어 헤쳐 오늘을 토해내고야 말았다'는 인생의 추운 겨울을 직면해야 하는 때를 직설적으로 표현한다. 그것은 '성탑을 쌓고/ 오늘을 보내'야 하는 고독과 단절의 시간이다. 하지만 시인의 긍정성은 이 어렵고 험난한 가운데서도 돌아온 마음과 떠나간 너의 마음이 원망이나 고통으로 표현되지 않는다. 돌아온 것도 떠나가는 것도 선한 순리의 물결로 이해되고 있기 때문이다. 이는 시간의 흐름이 계절의 순환으로 자연스럽게 받아들여지는 것과 마찬가지이다. 결국 화자는 '있으면 있는 대로' 없으면 없는 대로 '홀로 불씨 지펴 살아'가도 여전히 삶은 아름답다고 고백하고 있다.

이러한 화자의 긍정과 사랑의 원천이 오롯이 드러나는 시가 〈당신 있음에 · 1〉 〈당신 있음에 · 2〉가 있다.

아름다움과 그리움의 별들이
가득 찬 희망으로
사랑으로, 행복으로
하늘과 바다와 땅의 이름으로
가슴을 채울 수 있어
고개 들고 웃음으로 빛나는
당신 있음에

내 어찌 기뻐하지 않겠는가?

내 가슴 채울 수 있는 당신 앞에선
괴로움도 사치라 할 수 있어
홀로 이길 수 있는 연습도 하고
언제나 당신 앞에선 당당하게
삶의 의욕과 어떤 아픔도, 고난도, 비난도
함박꽃 웃음으로
찬란히 빛나리라.

- 〈당신 있음에 • 1〉

〈당신 있음에 ^ 1〉에서의 '당신'은 화자를 둘러싸고 있는 세상의 모든 것을 지칭한다. 그것은 하늘, 바다, 땅 같은 자연물이기도 하지만 내 주위에 있는 사랑하는 이들이기도 하다. 한 걸음 더 나아가 '당신'은 이 세상과 나를 존재하게 한 절대자이기도 하다. 화자에게는 세상에 존재하는 모든 것이 아름다움이며 그리움이기에 결국 그것은 사랑과 행복으로 귀결되는 순환의 구조를 가진다. 그렇다면 어떻게 화자는 〈봄꽃 여인〉의 시처럼 완전한 수용과 긍정으로 '마침내 꽃이 될' 수 있었던 것일까?

2연에서 보이듯 그대 앞에선 나의 괴로움조차 부끄러움이 된다. 그리하여 어떤 아픔도, 고난도, 비난도 당당하게 받아내며 굳게 설 것을 다짐한다. 하지만 화자는 그저 참는 것이 아니다. 그 인내의 끝에 무엇이 있는지 알기 때문에 과정의 고통을 기꺼이 감내하고자 하는 것이다. '함박꽃 웃음으로/ 찬란히 빛날' 것임을 알기에 가능한 일이다. 이는 화자가 의식하든 그렇지 않든 절대자에 대한 깊은 경외감의 발로가 아닐까!

"당신 있음에/ 내 어찌 기뻐하지 않겠는가?" 누가 감히 이토록 당당히 선언할 수 있는가? 그것은 화자의 흔들리지 않는 정체성에서 우러나오는 자신감이며, 절대자의 완전한 통치에 대한 무언의 확신이다. 깊은 내적 성숙에 이른 화자의 모습이 찬연하다.

당신이 있어 행복 꽃 피고
내가 있어 사랑 꽃 피어
일렁이는 창가에 기대어
마음속 얘기하며
꽃 필 수 있어 좋다.

마냥 가슴에 품고
행복 꽃, 사랑 꽃, 사랑의 비밀
고운 꽃 들판 당신 가슴 숨결처럼
가을로 올 수 있을까?

웃을 수 있는 고운 나비꽃처럼
예쁘고 아름다운 당신 가슴
하냥 행복 흐른다.

시간(時間)의 꽃을 가슴에 품고

행복 꽃, 사랑 꽃, 당신 가슴 숨결처럼
고운 꽃 들판 가을 향기 가득
꽃향기 가슴 피우리라.

<당신 있음에 · 2>

〈당신 있음에 · 1〉이 결연한 의지의 표현이었다면 〈당신 있음에 · 2〉는 합일의 지향이 드러난다. '당신'이 창조주이거나 나를 둘러싸고 있는 모든 타자(他者)이거나 상관없이 화자에게 '당신'은 함께 사랑, 행복을 꽃 피워야 할 존재이다. 화자는 창가에 기대어 설렘과 기대로 일렁이고 있다. '당신'의 가슴은 고운 꽃 들판으로 불어오는 숨결이기 때문이다. 고운 꽃 들판으로 형상화된 '당신'의 가슴은 광대함을 느끼게 한다. 한편에서 '숨결' '향기'라는 표현을 통해 부드러움과 섬세함이 살아난다. 그러므로 삶과 죽음이라는 절대성과 삶의 과정에서 일어나는 미묘한 아름다움으로까지 확장되어 시는 더욱 풍요롭게 다가온다.

〈당신 있음에〉와 조우할 수 있는 시가 〈님이시여, 때가 왔습니다〉이다. 다소 직설적이지만 제목 '님이시여, 때가 왔습니다'와 본문의 시가 보여주는 교감은 구조적 긴밀성을 만들어 내며 공명한다. '님이시여, 때가 왔습니다'의 이 당당한 선언은 〈당신 있음에 · 1〉에서 '당신 있음에/ 내 어찌 기뻐하지 않겠는가'와 맥을 같이하는 표현이다.

하지만 여기서 말하는 '때'는 만찬을 위해 준비된 그 '때'가 아니다. 사람이 성숙한다는 것, 또 강인함이란 어떤 것인지를 보여주는 시가 아닐까 한다. 삶이 얼마나 아름답고 살만한 것인지를 보여주는, 차라리

삶의 묘미가 가장 극명하게 드러나는 작품이라 말하면 어떨까?

지난봄부터 아픔이 오고
삶의 지혜가 필요했던 만큼
고뇌와 인내를 배우며
살아왔습니다.

고장 난 시계처럼 고치고 수리하며
아낌없이 구구절절이
사랑을 배웠습니다.

이제는 때가 왔습니다.

해결되지 않은 모든 문제에 대해
온몸으로 부딪히며
살아야 되리라는 것을
이제야 깨달았습니다.

조급하게 찾기보다
기도하며 기다리면
알찬 열매가 열린다는 것을!

문제 그 자체를 사랑하며
경험한다는 것은

행복이란 것을!

그러면 먼 훗날 자신도 모르게
기쁨이 온다는 것을!

아픔이 있기에 성장하고
참으로 행복이란 것을
알았습니다.

– 〈님이시여, 때가 왔습니다〉

결국 구구절절이 사랑을 배우는 때가 화자가 말하는 그'때'이다. 하지만 그것은 평탄함, 화려함, 성취 따위를 통해서가 아니라 고장 난 시계처럼 고치고 수리하는 일, 고뇌와 인내를 통해서다. 결국 모든 문제를 받아들이는 수용의 때를 화자는 기쁨으로 외치는 것이다. '님이시여, 때가 왔습니다'라고. 물아일체를 연상시킨다. 그러나 단순한 합일을 뛰어넘는 것은 이 과정을 성장으로 받아들이기 때문이다. 화자는 그러한 내면적인 성숙이야말로 진정 '행복'으로 인식한다. 사실 내면의 성숙이라는 말은 시인에게 부족한 표현이다. 시인은 대단히 영적인 사람이고 상당한 수준의 영적 교감과 성숙에 다다른 것처럼 보인다.
〈할미꽃〉을 살펴보자.

할미꽃 호박꽃
초롱불 밝히며

일어서는 세포들

인생의 지표
아직은 힘 있다.

볼 수 있고
쓸 수 있어
얼마나 즐거운지

생의 한 가운데
중심 기둥 되어
조심스레 불꽃 피운다.

- 〈할미꽃 · 1〉

애교 섞인 미소인데
저 매혹 시샘하다 핀
눈 흘기는 할미꽃!

다소곳이 고개 숙여
영접 받아
겸손한 할미꽃
고운 자태의 봄 햇살

귀여운 수줍음에
형형색색 모르는 게 많아
상식에 어설퍼
아쉬움에 웃고 있다.

    - 〈할미꽃 • 2〉

　이 시에서 할머니를 표상하는 꽃은 호박꽃이다. 화자는 볼 수 있고
쓸 수 있음에 감격한다. 하지만 누구나 나이가 들었다고 일상적인 것에
감사할 수 있는 것은 아니다. '상식에 어설퍼 아쉬움에 웃는' 화자의 겸
손한 태도의 발현이다. 죽음이 끝이라면 목적지가 가까워지는 도상에
서 감격하고 감사할 수 있을까? 무상함과 공허로움이 그를 사로잡거나
체념하지 않을까. 체념과 무상함은 사물에 대한 변별성을 잃게 한다.
오늘이 어제 같고 만사가 빛을 잃어버린다. 그곳에 새로움은 존재하지
않는다.
　하지만 화자는 여전히 초롱불을 밝히고 인생의 지표를 향해 나아가
고 있다. 인생의 여로(旅路)에서 반평생도 훌쩍 지나버린 이 나이에도
'생의 한 가운데' 있는 이유이다. 마치 죽음의 순간까지도 한 그루 사과
나무를 심겠다는 결기로 삶을 자연스럽게 발화하고 있다.

　〈불면의 가을밤 사이로〉는 언어의 결이 아름답고 장엄하다. 마치 교
향곡을 듣고 있는 듯 하나의 서사를 완성해 내고 있다.
　밥이 보약, 잠이 보약이다. 지친 몸과 마음이 숙면을 통해 회복된다.
숙면 후 깨어났을 때 몸은 얼마나 개운하고 맑아지는 것일까? 혼미하

던 모든 것이 명징해진다. 그렇기에 때로 밥보다 잠이 더 보약일 때가 많다. 그런 의미에서 '불면증'이란 과히 좋은 어감으로 와 닿지 않는다. 시인은 불면증까지는 아닐지라도 식은땀이 등줄기를 타고 흘러내리는 불면의 밤을 보내고 있다. 하지만 시인은 이 불면의 밤을 달리 해석하고 받아들이기로 한다. 그럴 때 불면의 밤은 오묘하게 새싹을 돋아내며 이야기를 쏟아낸다. 결국 '불면을 일으켜 세우는/ 금빛 수런거림에' 온밤을 새우고 '눈 비비며 깨어나는 햇살'을 마주하는 것이다. 〈불면의 가을밤 사이로〉에서 마지막 연 '파다닥 열린 가슴으로'에서 '파다닥'은 살짝 놀라 서두르는 모습과 펄럭거리는 날갯짓의 소리로 중첩적으로 이해되며 떠오르는 햇살 위로 유유히 날아가는 새의 모습이 연상된다.

고요가 세상(世上)을 넘칠 때

불면(不眠)을 일으켜 세우는
금빛 언어들의 수런거림에
등줄기를 타고 흘러내리는 식은 땀!

진한 커피 한 잔에
머리를 식혀
입안 가득
가을을 몰고 온다.

하늘에서 하늘로
거리에서 거리로

온몸 흔들며 쏟아져 내리는

고독의 한 줄기 몸 안 가득 받아

뾰족뾰족 솟아나는 가을 새싹들처럼

그리운 꿈 향해

설렘 속 사랑으로

눈 비비며 깨어나는 햇살 한 아름

파다닥 열린 가슴으로

노랠 부른다.

    – 〈불면의 가을밤 사이로〉

시인의 언어적인 아름다움은 기존의 상식을 뒤엎어 탄생한다.

이렇듯 시인의 언어의 비범성을 드러내는 시편 중 하나는 〈고향산천 그리워〉이다. 의식의 흐름이 뛰어난 가시성으로 형상화되어 있다. 산들 바람처럼 살랑이며 또 휘몰아 오는 풍경은 시인의 놀라운 언어의 직조 술에 의한 것이다. '추억의 푸념은/ 예정 없이/ 하루를 서성이다… 종달 새 울음/ 그 언덕에도 애꿎은/ 상념만 보내고// 커다랗게 피어난/ 들풀 의 흔들거림이/ 마지막 인사치레로/ 넘실댄다 …' 즉 〈고향산천 그리워 〉는 형상과 관념, 가시와 불가시, 추상과 구체성의 개념을 허물며 언어 의 새로운 차원을 개척해 내고 있다. 뿐만 아니라 바래지 않는 고향의 아늑한 정서가 '마지막 인사치레' '세월의 무게'에도 깊은 안도감으로 들풀의 한들거림에 실려온다. 언어의 결이 살아 너울거린다.

아련한 추억의 푸념은
예정 없이
하루를 꼬박 서성이다
지친 듯

종달새 울음
그 언덕에도 애꿎은
상념만 보내고 나니

커다랗게 피어난
들풀의 흔들거림이
마지막 인사치레로
넘실댄다.

그리움은 핑계처럼 돌아가버리고
세월의 무게들만 라일락 잎새
스치듯 휘어돌아
묵은 피를 토해내고

흔적을 찾아
빗방울에 실어봅니다.

- 〈고향산천 그리워〉

삶의 저력을 가진 이들은 애착하는 것이 많다. 무엇인가를 귀하게 여기고 소중히 간직한다. 이는 사람과의 관계에 있어서도 동일하다. 동시대뿐만 아니라 역사적 인물에 대한 존경을 가지며 교감하는 경우가 그렇다. 이들의 삶의 지평은 넓고 단단하다. 든든히 뿌리를 내린 이들은 크고 작은 일에 요동하지 않으며 가치 있는 선택으로 미래를 향해 뻗어나간다.

시의 부제처럼 '천년의 꽃'으로 〈열여덟 유관순 열사의 그날은〉은 유관순 열사를 애통하고도 숭고하게 한편은 처절하게 피워내고 있다. 그날의 흔적을 따라가며 핏빛 절규로 붉다. '마디마디 울어서 퉁퉁 부은' 유관순 열사의 희생은 나라 안에 있는 한 영혼 한 영혼에 대한 사랑이었으리. 열여덟의 처자가 고개를 떨군 자리에 대한의 오천만 생명이 움을 틔웠다. 시 〈물 향기 수목원〉에서 '가슴에 달고 계시는 엄마를'이라는 표현처럼 온 국민이 가슴에 달아야 할 꽃이 유관순 열사가 아닌가?

핏빛 절규가 온 국민의 가슴을 붉게 물들인다. 장엄하다.

유관순, 그녀가 가던 그날은
하늘이 슬피 울고 땅도 울고
새들도 울었다.

일천구백일십구년 삼월 봄부터 이듬해 구월까지
열여덟 순국선열 유관순, 그녀는
대한독립만세! 피맺힌 절규! 절규!

온통 울음바다, 그치지 않고

마디마디 울어서 퉁퉁 부어 있었다.
못다 핀 꽃 유관순 열사, 대한독립만세!
부르짖다 간 청춘의 넋이여!

그녀가 가던 그날의 눈물이 너무 젖어
압록강 한강 낙동강 빨갛게 타올라
철철 넘쳐흘러 마침내 광복절의 해방!

민족의 가슴에는 사랑으로 희망으로
천년의 꽃이 되어 하늘 동산에
길이길이 피어났다.

　　- 〈열여덟 유관순 열사의 그날은〉
　　　　-천년의 꽃-

　아름다움이란 무엇일까? 처음엔 경이로 바라보던 어떤 것들도 시간
이 지나면서 그 아름다움은 빛을 잃어버리고 퇴색해지기 마련이다. 그
리하여 경탄에 마지않던 것들도 흔하고 일상적인 것으로 화(化)한다.
습관적인 눈과 굳어진 마음에서는 새로울 것이 없다. 마음에 담을 귀
하고 소중한 것도 발견하기 어렵다.
　시인이란 무엇일까? 마치 숨겨진 보석을 찾는 것처럼 일상에 묻힌
삶의 아름다움을 발견하고 그 경이로움을 노래하는 이가 아닐까.
　그렇다. 시인 권영주의 시들은 무서우리만치 삶의 아름다움과 경이
로움에 천착(穿鑿)하고 있다. 그것은 일상의 연속선상에서 사물을 보

는 것이 아니라 매 순간을 마치 전부인 것처럼, 마지막인 것처럼 받아들이는 '신선함'을 모태로 한다. 영화 필름의 한 컷 한 컷을 스틸영상으로 보는 것처럼 시인에게 있어서 삶이란 그저 흘러가는 것이 아니라 고요하게 파도치며 시인의 가슴으로 밀려오는 것이다.

이렇듯 삶의 아름다움을 온전히 느끼며 노래할 수 있는 것은 무엇보다 흔들리지 않는 강인한 정신력에서 비롯되고 있다. 단지 감성이 풍부하다는 것만으로는 외적인 아름다움의 피상성(皮相性)을 넘어서 내적인 자아의 확장으로 나아가기는 쉽지 않다. 권영주 시인의 시는 삶의 깊은 철학과 실천이 내면화되어 있는 성장과 성숙으로 귀착되는 여로이기도 하다.

그런 의미에서 평자는 그의 시가 많은 이에게, 특별히 청소년들의 애송시가 되기를 바란다. 똑같은 현상을 두고 십인십색, 다 다른 결론에 이른다. 하지만 내면의 힘이 찬연한 생명력으로 발화하는 지점으로 돌아가, 어떻게 삶을 아름답게 피워내는지를 배우는 것은 흙 속에 묻힌 진주를 발견할 수 있는 삶의 안목과 통찰을 얻는 것이다. 이는 삶의 여로(旅路)에서 진정 가치 있는 열매를 맺는 가장 빠른 지름길일 것이다. 우리 인생은 정체되고 허비될 수 없다. 삶의 시간마다 다른 지평의 아름다움을 누려야 하고 색다른 역할들에서 더욱 단단하게 성숙해져야 하기 때문이다.

시집 『물 향기 수목원』은 삶의 원숙한 아름다움이 물빛 언어로 반짝인다.

* 천착(穿鑿): 학문을 깊이 연구함

At Last, Becoming a Flower

Shaping the Inner Strength
and the Beauty in a New Language

Lee Chul-ho (Novelist, Literary Critic)

Language represents the person. Perhaps language is the person itself. Because we think and communicate through it, language inevitably reflects who we are. It also shapes us, for thought arises only through language. Thought is always revealed in life in one form or another. Though unseen, language has its own world and shapes values for both individual and society. During President Yoon Suk-yeol's martial law declaration, the word most often repeated was 'frame.' (Politics, after all, is often called a war of frames.) Here, the frame bore the force of a mold.

Why invoke politics and frames at this point? For language itself can become a prison, yet it can also unfold as the wings of 'freedom'—"You will know the truth, and the truth will set you free" (John 8:32).

Poet Kwon Young-joo shows a genius for reinterpreting and applying the dimensions of language. In her work, experimental attempts that overturn familiar perceptions of words settle with high completeness, creating beauty of form. With imagery that dissolves linguistic boundaries and emotions that drift in like a breeze, each poem reaches a peak of artistic expression.

What deepens the power of her poetry is the inner strength rooted in her way of life. To prize the maturity of character as the highest value may seem unusual in an age that dismisses nobility and grace. Yet the poet is unmoved by the world's gaze, simply savoring the beauty found along her path. The collection *Arboretum of Water Fragrance* shows this strength and tells the story of 'a woman who has at last become a flower.'

First, "Arboretum of Water Fragrance" shines with ripples of lights in deep reassurance. Though layered since long ago, this longing holds no staleness or sorrow. Its radiance comes from opening the window of yearning, like polishing 'a rusted mirror,' to meet its object and the renew memory. Thus the memory grows warm again, like a freshly baked bread.

Kwon's poetry is marked by emotional warmth, yet without the roughness or rusticity the words might suggest. Like the Adonis Flower breaking through ice after a harsh winter, her warmth is vivid and alive. If the guiding emotion of her work is the mystery and awe of life's first birth, the poem "Arboretum of Water Fragrance" embodies it fully.

What, then, is the 'water fragrance' as it talks of in "Arboretum of Water Fragrance"? It is surely not the smell of the sea, for no forest grows upon a mudflat. Perhaps it is the pungent yet unsalty freshness of fresh water where creatures swim. In any case, it suggests the primal waters that nurture life, the fragrance of bubbling springs. Joined with 'water fragrance,' the arboretum carries a dual sense: not only a garden of trees (樹木園) but also of water and trees (水木園).

The road I take at last to visit you

The sunlight tender the wind fair

The sunlight too catching its breath

Crosses the river of the seasons

The road I take at last to visit you

Weeping willows azaleas quince blossoms

I hide

Wind in my left pocket

Flower of laughter in my right

When spring sunlight pours I draw them forth

Into the mountains where azaleas smile

With my mother I climb

259

The opening line, 'The road I take at last to visit you,' is simple yet deeply moving, carrying a quiet warmth rather than urgent longing. "The sunlight too catching its breath / Crosses the river of the seasons" gives shape to this long absence, suggesting hardship yet rendered luminous through sunlight. Thus at last conveys not sorrow but the gladness of meeting again. The lines "Weeping willows azaleas quince blossoms / Wind in my left pocket / Flower of laughter in my right" add rhythm and fairy-tale imagery, lightening the weight of mystery and joining reality with imagination.

The latter part of the poem recalls the warmth and beauty of being with the mother in spring sunlight. Thus "The road I take at last to visit you" is also the road back to those memories. The dishes and rice prepared with "The glittering spring sunlight" are what she longs for, revealing that her strength lies in warmth itself. Love and memory continue to radiate within, giving her power to overcome hardships and cold. A simple example of this may be seen in "Winter Mountain".

Winds at every branch joint unraveled
At last spat out today!

Like a heart that had returned
O heart that departed from me
Waves that live in light

I too have built a tower in my chest
And now I send off the day
With a voice gone hoarse.

If it is there it is as it is
The mountain remains silent
Forgetting spring, summer, and autumn
Alone kindling embers and
Going on with life.

- Winter Mountain

The lines "Winds at every branch joint / Unraveled the long forgotten stories / That had piled up and at last spat out today" speak directly of life's cold winter. It is the solitude of having to "build a tower in my chest / And now send off the day." Yet neither the heart that returned nor the heart that departed is expressed as pain, but as waves that live in light, part of life's natural flow. Thus, with the words 'If it is there it is as it is' and 'alone kindling embers and going on with life,' the speaker affirms that life remains beautiful.

The poems "Because You Are • 1" and "Because You Are • 2" most fully reveal the source of the speaker's affirmation and love.

Stars of beauty and longing

Brimming with hope

With love, with happiness

In the name of sky sea and earth

My heart can be filled

With your head lifted shining in a smile

Because you are here

How could I not rejoice?

Before you who can fill my heart

Even sorrow could be called a luxury

I practice to endure alone

In "Because You Are • 1", the 'You' embraces all that surrounds the speaker—the sky, sea, earth, loved ones, and even the Absolute who grants existence. For the speaker, all things turn into beauty and longing, returning in a cycle of love and happiness. Through this acceptance, the poet, as in "Lady of Spring Blossom", can 'at last become a flower.'

As the second stanza shows, even the speaker's sorrow becomes shame before the beloved. Thus the speaker resolves to face every pain, hardship, and blame with dignity. Yet this is not mere endurance; it is the willingness to bear suffering because the end is known—"With a radiant smile / I will shine brilliantly." Such confidence reflects, consciously or not, a deep reverence for the Absolute. "Because you are here / How could I not rejoice?"—who could dare to declare this so boldly? It is confidence arising from an unshaken identity and a silent trust in the Absolute's perfect rule. Here the image of the speaker's inner maturity shines resplendent.

Because of you flowers of happiness bloom

Because of me flowers of love bloom

Leaning by the shimmering window

Blooming with cheerful talk

Whispered from my heart.

Holding close within my heart

Flowers of happiness, flowers of love, the secret of love

A gentle field of blossoms like the breath in your chest

Could it return again as autumn?

Like a graceful butterfly-flower smiling

Your heart so lovely and beautiful

Lets happiness flow without end.

With the flowers of time held to my heart

Flowers of happiness, flowers of love, like the breath in your chest

In a gentle field filled with autumn fragrance

The scent of blossoms will bloom in my heart.

- Because You Are • 2

If "Because You Are • 1" expresses resolute will, "Because You

Are • 2" turns toward union. Whether the 'You' is Creator or companion, 'You' is the one with whom love and happiness must bloom. Leaning by the window, the speaker stirs with anticipation, for "Your heart is the breath that drifts in from a gentle field of flowers." This image conveys vastness, yet through 'breath' and 'fragrance' it also breathes softness. Thus the poem expands from life and death to the subtle beauties of existence, and reaches the reader with greater richness.

The poem "Because You Are" finds its counterpart in "Beloved, the Time Has Come" The resolute title "Beloved, the Time Has Come' resonates with "Because You Are • 1": "Because you are here / How could I not rejoice?" Yet the "Time" here is not the banquet prepared and waiting but the time of ripening and of learning strength. As the poet declares in "Beloved, the Time Has Come": "Now the time has come / For every unresolved problem / I must face it / With my whole being." Together these poems reveal that through pain comes growth and through endurance, joy—showing most vividly the beauty and savor of life.

Since last spring pain has come and

As much as I needed the wisdom of life

I have lived

Learning anguish and patience.

Like a broken clock mended and repaired
Without holding back in every detail
I have learned love.

Now the time has come.

For every unresolved problem
I have realized at last
That I must face it
With my whole being.

Rather than seeking in haste
If I pray and wait
I will see fruitful harvests!

To love the problem itself
To experience it
Is to know happiness!

And then, in a far-off tomorrow
Without knowing how joy will come!

Because there is pain, there is growth
And I have come to know

That this, truly is happiness.

- Beloved, the Time Has Come

The 'Time' the speaker proclaims is the season of learning love in every detail. Yet it comes not through ease or achievement, but through anguish and patience—"Like a broken clock mended and repaired." The moment of acceptance, "Now the time has come / For every unresolved problem, / I have realized at last / That I must face it / With my whole being," is lifted as joy. To "Love the problem itself, / To experience it, / Is to know happiness" is to see suffering itself as growth. Happiness here is not mere endurance but the sign of deep spiritual maturity. The poet appears to have entered into a higher communion of spirit. Let us turn to Pasqueflower.

Pasqueflower Pumpkin flower
Cells rise
Like lanterns lit

Life's compass
Still holds its strength.

To be able to see and
To be able to write

How joyful it is

In the midst of life
As a central pillar
Carefully blossoms into flames.

- Pasqueflower • 1

With a smile tinged with charm
Blooming in envy of allure
A side-glancing Pasqueflower!

Bowing its head modestly
Welcoming with humility
The Pasqueflower
Graceful in the spring sunlight

In its shy cuteness
So much unknown in many colors
Awkward in common sense
Smiles a wistful smile.

- Pasqueflower • 2

Here the flower that represents the grandmother is the pumpkin flower. The speaker is moved with gratitude simply "To be able to see and / To be able to write / How joyful it is." And yet such thankfulness for the ordinary is not common in old age; it reflects the humility of one who is 'awkward in common sense, laughing at regret.' But if death is the end, could one still feel such gratitude? Would not impermanence and emptiness press toward resignation, where today is the same as yesterday and all things lose their light? In such a place, newness cannot exist.

Yet the speaker still lights a lantern and moves toward life's compass. Even at an age where more than half of life's journey has already slipped by, this is why she remains 'in the midst of life.' The determination to plant an apple tree even at the very brink of death emerges naturally as an expression of life itself.

"Through a Sleepless Autumn Night" unfolds with solemn beauty, like a symphony completing its narrative.

Food and sleep are both medicine, yet at times sleep proves the greater cure, clearing body and mind after waking. Though the poet may not suffer true insomnia, she spends restless nights with cold sweat along her spine. However, by embracing these nights, she lets them sprout into stories, staying awake through "the rustling of golden words that stir my sleepless night" until she meets "a handful of sunlight rubs its eyes awake." Such sleepless hours, rather than mere suffering, become the fertile ground for language and imagination. The poem reveals how even fatigue can turn into renewal when accepted with openness. In the final line, "with wings bursting from my chest" suggests both a startled flutter and the beating of wings, evoking a bird soaring into the rising sun.

With love in trembling excitement

A handful of sunlight rubs its eyes awake

And with a chest thrown open like wings

Sings its song.

- Through a Sleepless Autumn Night

The beauty of the poet's language is born from overturning convention.

"Longing for My Hometown" reveals the poet's exceptional command of language. The flow of consciousness takes vivid form, and the shifting breeze-like scenes are woven by a rare craftsmanship. Lines such as "The rambling lament of the faded memories … The wide blooming sway of / Wild grass ripples / In a final gesture of farewell" collapse the boundaries of form and idea, visible and invisible, abstract and concrete, opening a new dimension of expression. Moreover, the unfading warmth of home is carried in the swaying grass, bringing calm even amid 'a final gesture of farewell' and 'the weight of years.' The texture of language comes alive, rippling with life.

The rambling lament of the faded memories

Unplanned

Has me wandering all day

And

I let it go as if worn out

The lark's cry

Even on that hill

Only sends off pointless thoughts

The wide blooming sway of

Wild grass ripples

In a final gesture of farewell

Longing turns back like an excuse

And only the weight of years

Brushes past lilac leaves in a winding arc

Spits out the clotted blood

In search of traces

I set them afloat on raindrops

- Longing for My Hometown

Those who carry resilience in life cherish what is precious and keep it close to heart. This holds true not only in their bonds with others but also in the respect they extend to the figures of the past. With horizons both wide and firm, they are deeply rooted, not easily shaken, and move steadily toward the future through choices of enduring value.

Like its subtitle "A Thousand-Year Flower, The Day of Eighteen-Year-Old Martyr Yoo Gwan-sun" mourns and exalts her with reverence and sorrow. The poem burns with blood-red cries: "Every joint, swelling with each sob, / Her body bruised and swollen / Yoo Gwan-sun, the flower that could not fully bloom …" Her sacrifice shines as love for the nation, and where the bowed head of an eighteen-year-old once lay, countless lives of Korea sprang forth. As in "Arboretum of Water Fragrance" with the words 'the mother you wear upon your chest,' so too must the people wear Yoo Gwan-sun upon their hearts. Her blood-sealed cry dyes the nation crimson—majestic indeed.

Yoo Gwan-sun,

On the day she bid her last farewell

The sky wept the earth wept and

Even the birds wept.

From the spring of March 1919

To the September of the following year

Eighteen-year-old martyr Yoo Gwan-sun

Her cry her blood-sealed cry

Long live Korean independence!

A cry soaked in blood a cry!

A flood of sorrow never ceasing

Every joint swelling with each sob.

Her body bruised and swollen

Yoo Gwan-sun, the flower that could not fully bloom

O soul of youth gone shouting Long live Korean independence!

The tears of the day she left this tear soaked land

Turning the Amnok River the Han River and

The Nakdong River burning red

Overflowing until at last came the Liberation Day of freedom!

In the heart of the nation as love and as hope

She became a flower of the Thousand Years

Forever blooming

In the heavenly garden.

- The Day of Eighteen-Year-Old Martyr Yoo Gwan-sun

-A Thousand-Year Flower-

What is beauty? With time, even what once amazed us loses its glow and turns ordinary. Eyes dulled by habits and hearts grown rigid no longer see what is new, making it harder to discover what is truly precious.

What is a poet? It is not one who uncovers hidden beauty in ordinary life and sings of its wonder.

Indeed, Kwon Young-joo's poems delve into the beauty and the wonders of life. Their freshness comes not from seeing things as part of a continuum, but from embracing each moment as if it were the whole and the last, like watching each frame of a film as a still image. For the poet, life does not simply pass by; it rolls in like quiet waves, pressing upon the heart.

The ability to fully feel and sing of life's beauty springs above all from an unshaken strength of spirit. Mere richness of emotion alone cannot move beyond the superficiality of outer beauty to the expansion of the inner self. Kwon's poetry is also a journey of growth and maturity, where deep philosophy and practice in life are inwardly embodied.

In this sense, I hope her poems will become beloved by many, especially the young. Faced with the same reality, ten people may reach ten different conclusions, yet to return to the point where the inner strength bursts forth with radiant vitality is to learn how life can blossom beautifully, gaining the insight to find the pearls hidden in the soil. This is the surest path to bearing fruits of true worth. Our lives cannot remain stagnant nor be wasted; we must continually discover the new horizons of beauty and grow stronger through the varied roles life gives us.

The poetry collection *Arboretum of Water Fragrance* sparkles with the mature beauty of life in the language glowing with water's light.

마음 설레는 새해의 문이 막 열렸다.

지난해 수개월에 걸쳐 한 편 한 편 다른 언어꽃으로 피어난 권영주 시인의 시들이 한 아름 예쁜 리본에 묶여 독자들에게 선보일 준비를 서두르고 있다.

1년여 전 권영주 시인으로부터 번역 의뢰 차 전화를 받았다. 오랜 친구에게서 걸려 온 전화 같았다.

그녀는 한국문인 연수원 교수로, 나는 번역위원으로 위촉장 수여식에 참가하였을 때 처음 만난 것이 인연의 전부로 잊힐 만한 세월이 흘렀지만 그녀를 처음 만났던 기억이 또렷한 이유가 뭘까.

그때 몇 마디 나누던 중 우리가 동갑내기인 것을 알게 되었고, 나는 내심 꽤 놀라워했던 것 같다. 그녀는 이삼십 대에게나 가능한 긴 머리와 호리호리한 몸매와 청초함까지 지니고 있었다. 경상도 말씨에서 애교도 느껴졌다. 앞으로 자신의 시를 번역하고 싶고, 준비가 되면 연락하고 싶다고 했다. 나는 그녀의 시도 그녀를 닮았을까 궁금했었다.

그녀는 잊지 않고 연락을 해왔다. 궁금했던 그녀의 시들 역시 여림과 지순함과 인내 속 강인함의 감성들로 어우러져 있다. 눈 녹은 자리에 뾰족이 시린 얼굴을 내민 제비꽃처럼 이 시집이 새봄에 태어나길 고대하며 매일매일 부지런히 번역작업에 임했다.

기쁘게 번역할 수 있는 기회를 준 저자께 진심으로 감사하며 건강과 문운을 기원합니다.

아울러 나의 번역에 완성도와 아름다움을 더해주는 그레이 감수자께도 감사와 사랑을 전합니다.

2026년 새해를 맞이하며
역자 라이채

The gates of the New Year have just opened, stirring my heart with anticipation.

Over several months last year, the poems of poet Kwon Young-Joo have bloomed one by one as blossoms of another language, now tied together with a beautiful ribbon and are ready to be presented to readers.

About a year ago, I received a phone call from her requesting translation. It felt like a call from an old friend.

We first met at a ceremony where she was appointed as a professor and I as a translation committee member at the Korea Writers' Training Institute. Quite some time has passed since then, perhaps enough for it to be forgotten, yet the memory of our first meeting remains vivid.

In those brief exchanges, I discovered we were the same age—something that surprised me. She carried the long hair, slender figure, and quiet freshness usually seen only in one's twenties or thirties, even with a touch of charm in her Gyeongsang-do accent. She mentioned she hoped to have her poems translated someday and would reach out when she was ready. I remember wondering then whether her poetry might resemble her.

And true to her word, she called. Her poems turned out to be just as I had imagined—woven with gentleness, purity, and a quiet strength within patience. Each day, I worked diligently, longing for this collection to be born in the new spring, like violets pricking their cold faces from the thawing ground.

I offer my sincere gratitude to the author for granting me the joy of this translation, and I wish her health and continued literary fortune.

My thanks and affection also go to Suk Grey, my proofreader, who has enriched my translation with completeness and beauty.

At the threshold of the New Year 2026,

Translator Eechae Ra

라이채

· 번역문학가 국제 펜 한국본부 회원

· 문예지 「문학 수」 번역위원 및 번역 심사위원.

· 종합문예지 「한국문인」 편집주간 및 번역책임자 역임.

· 덕성여대 영어영문과 졸업. 미연방한의사.

· 「세상의 빛 어머니 사랑」, 「독도 사랑」(영역), 「하프 라이프」(국역) 외, 다수의 영한 대역 서와 「수필의 끈을 풀다」 외 다수의 공동 작품집이 있다.

· 한국문인번역문학상 본상 수상.

· 이메일: isakok@hanmail.net

Eechae Ra

· Translator & Writer.

· Member of the Korean Centre of International PEN.

· Translation Committee Member and Judge for the literary journal *Munhak Su*.

· Former Managing Editor and Head of Translation at the *Korea Writers*.

· Graduate from the Department of English Language and Literature, Duksung Women's University.

· Certified Doctor of Oriental Medicine in the United States.

· Published works include numerous bilingual Korean–English editions such as *The Light of the World, Mother's Love, Love for Dokdo*, and *Half Life*(Korean edition), along with collaborative essay collections including *Unraveling the Ties of the Essay.*

· Recipient of the Korea Writers' Literary Translation Grand Award.